Toto Reveals the True Story

Dennis Sanchez

Published by Dennis Sanchez, 2024.

This is a work of fiction. Similarities to real people, places, or events are entirely coincidental.

TOTO REVEALS THE TRUE STORY

First edition. September 7, 2024.

ISBN: 979-8227781239

Written by Dennis Sanchez.

Also by Dennis Sanchez

Mystery of the Missing Parents
Mystery of the Man in the Mirror
Toto Reveals the True Story

Watch for more at https://damfinowriter.webnode.com/.

Table of Contents

To my wife, Kate, for all the years of unyielding loving support

FACT OF THE MATTER

L. Frank Baum got it all wrong. Well, I will give him credit for depicting the events in the Land of Oz as best as he could and in the order that they occurred. However, the author disregarded the one true hero of the tale. The one who guided the others through perilous lands and saved them from one mishap after another with cunning, ingenuity, and bravery. I know this because I am that hero. Toto is the name.

Maybe it is the fact that L. Frank Baum, as he researched the adventure, could not grasp my Cairn terrier accent, which made him compelled to focus on my companions' involvement, practically leaving me out altogether. I can't blame him for not understanding me; no one else in this whole adventure understood a single bark I made, no matter how distinctly I enunciated myself.

Putting that aside I, now in my later years, have decided to correct and amend the tale and tell it as it truly happened.

IT BEGAN ONE EARLY morning while we were all standing out on the porch; that is Dorothy, Uncle Henry, Aunt Em, and I. We stood there gazing at nothing in particular because there is little to look at in this barren, drab, flat land of Kansas. Suddenly, the sky turned dark, really dark. My fur stuck straight up and I knew something was amiss. With a few loud barks, I gave the warning that there was a storm heading our way. A big and powerful storm. However, Dorothy, Aunt Em, and Uncle Henry ignored me and simply told me to hush, possibly because I was interrupting their characteristic moments of mindless gazing with something they might have to ponder.

As the sky grew darker and darker and the wind pressed hard against us, Uncle Henry turned his gaze skyward.

"Hmm," he grumbled his concern, his face frozen in a constant state of tedium.

"Hmm," agreed Aunt Em, looking up in the opposite direction, expressionless.

"Hmm?" asked Dorothy, wide-eyed, and befuddled. She glanced in all directions, not understanding.

A whirling, twirling black funnel cloud headed our way, and I gritted my teeth and growled under my breath. The funnel cloud turned the countryside even more drab than before as it sucked up everything in its path. Cyclone they called it and it was gigantic. Miles across at the top and narrowing to a quarter of a mile where it touched the ground. As the cyclone scraped the Earth farmhouses, barns, and silos were splintered into matchsticks. Tractors, trailers, combines, even people and livestock, were sucked up into it, and round and round they rode inside of it. Some of the debris, including animals and people, broke free and could be seen hurtling in all directions.

"Ruff-ruff-ruff," I said, detailing the devastation and identifying the cause behind it.

"Cyclone," Uncle Henry stated in his typical offhanded way.

"Cyclone," Aunt Em gave a solemn nod.

"Cyclone?" asked Dorothy, as always clueless.

Without a word, Uncle Henry ran off like a madman toward the barn, leaving the three of us behind on the porch. More concerned about the livestock than us. I could understand his reasoning if there were dogs in there. Or cats, maybe, but not simply for the sake of edible livestock. Livestock is simple-minded and uninteresting, unlike us dogs.

Just as suddenly, Aunt Em freaked out, ran into the house, opened a door in the middle of the floor, and jumped down into a hole in the ground. Pretty much looking after herself. Well, I have to admit I got a little nervous, but Dorothy just stood there staring at the cyclone coming at us fast. I got up on my hind legs, snapped my jaws on the hem of her dress, and pulled her backward into the house, but Dorothy was not helping much. I pulled, hopping on my hind legs while Dorothy dragged her feet, her gaze on the cyclone unrelenting. I had managed to pull her into the middle of the house when there was this loud, shrieking noise and the house shuddered so hard it knocked Dorothy and I to the floor. The house began to turn in circles and it started to rise, and up we went. I didn't like it. Not one barking bit. The house tilted as it spun, and I slid into the open hole in the middle of the floor, but the ground below and Aunt Em were no longer there. It was just space beneath our house. A whole lot of space. Fortunately, the wind, very fast and whirling, kept me afloat or I would have fallen miles back to earth. Dorothy pulled me out of the hole by my ear and slammed the door shut before I fell away. I do have to admit that it scared me because I knew we had risen higher than any rainbow.

The house continued to spin and tilt one way and then the other and we got so dizzy and tired that we both jumped up on her bed and fell asleep.

Think that's strange, you won't believe what happened next.

LANDING

Bam!

Even though we came down hard, our landing was still rather gentle for a cyclone-carried house. Anyway, the landing woke me with a start and I yelped and dug my cold nose in Dorothy's face, quivering. Ah, not from fear, mind you. Quivering from the cold. It was a bit nippy inside the house, you see. Yeah, well... I felt Dorothy's hand rubbing my back. I let her rub my back all she wanted because I knew it made her feel a little safer and more secure.

After a short while, I realized it wasn't as dark and drab as before. A strange, bright, warm sunlight now filled the windows. Brighter and warmer sunlight than I ever remember seeing and feeling in Kansas.

Dorothy jumped up and ran to the door and I was quick on her heels. As she swung the door open, I was astounded to see a land more beautiful than I had ever seen before. There were trees... big, soaring trees! My little feet stomped for joy, but my attention soon turned to the succulent fruit, budding flowers, fluttering and chirping birds, and clean, clear water rushing down a brook between banks of sprouting foliage. A big improvement over the dull, drab, flat prairies we left behind in Kansas. I could swear, too, I heard music and high-pitched singing, but it seemed more in the distant background.

I turned my gaze up at Dorothy and we exchanged glances, our eyes wide with wonder. I barked, "Gosh, I don't think we're still in Kansas," but all she said was, "Hush, Toto." This happened a lot when I try to express myself to anyone other than fellow dogs.

Then appearing from behind every bush, rock, and tree were the oddest-looking people. At least a hundred of them. They wore pointed hats that towered a foot over their heads, and around the brims were tinkling bells.

Dorothy pointed, "Look, Toto. They are all dressed in blue, from their hats down to their shoes."

They also looked to be around Uncle Henry's and Aunt Em's age. They were huge, too. Almost as big as Dorothy, who is a good-sized girl for her age. Yeah, I know, all humans are huge compared to me, but that's not the point.

They drew nearer but stopped short of us and whispered among themselves. Then, out of the crowd came an old woman with long, straight hair and a wrinkled-up face but dressed differently than the others. She wore a pleated, flowing gown with little stars that twinkled in the sunlight. The gown lacked any real color so I guess it must be what Dorothy often called white.

The woman walked stiffly up to where we stood on the porch and bent forward at the waist. I stiffened and growled, but not so loud as to attract too much attention because there were so many of them watching from a distance with curiosity.

The woman in white spoke in a sweet tone of voice and said, "Oh, noble Sorceress, you have killed the Wicked Witch of the East and freed the Munchkins from bondage and for this we are grateful."

Dorothy answered, somewhat bewildered, "Oh-my, but there must be some mistake. I have only arrived and have killed no one."

I stepped toward the woman and growled in agreement.

The woman in white looked down at me a moment, smiled, and then shoved me aside with the pointy toe of her shoe and answered, "You may not have directly, but your house did. Look for yourself."

I scampered off the porch with Dorothy and saw two legs with sparkly shoes on their feet sticking out from under the house. There was little space between the ground and the bottom of the house so whoever was under there had to be flat as a pancake. To be certain this person was dead, I sniffed and licked the soles of the shoes, but got no response.

I looked up at Dorothy and saw that she had put her hands to her cheeks and said in a worried shriek, "Oh my! I certainly didn't do it on purpose." Then, in a sudden change in demeanor, Dorothy narrowed her eyes on the woman in white. With her body stiffened and hands placed on her hips in a defiant posture, she added, "Look here, if you are accusing me of murder, the ol' witch had no right to be standing under a house falling from the sky no matter who occupied it." She wagged a finger in the woman in white's face to emphasize the point.

The woman in white responded with a pleasant smile, "Calm down, Honeybunch. No need to get your feathers all ruffled. In the first place, the Munchkins didn't particularly care for the ol' b... I mean, witch, and in the second place, they are grateful that someone finally took the necessary steps to do away with her. A novel form of execution, but effective."

"These Munchkins, who are they?" asked Dorothy, her demeanor swinging effortlessly back to perkiness as she looked behind the woman in white at all the strange people inching in masse closer and closer.

The woman in white, while waving a silvery stick with a little knob at one end that sprouted tiny shooting stars, answered, "These are the people of the East who, until now, were under the rule of this Wicked Witch you have killed."

"Are you a Munchkin?" asked Dorothy.

"Oh, no," the woman said, waving her stick in greater and greater circles.

I kept a keen eye on that stick, waiting for her to launch it so I could retrieve it, but to my dismay, she held on to it with a tight grip.

"I am the Good Witch of the North and I came at once when the Munchkins got such joyous word to me that the Wicked Witch of the East was dead."

Dorothy again put both hands to her cheeks and, in astonishment, she said, "Gee, you're a witch, too?"

"Who else would go around carrying a silvery stick with a little knob at one end that sprouts tiny shooting stars?" said the Good Witch of the North, her high-pitched voice squeaking with pride. "I've been in the witch trade for more than three thousand years."

"If you're a witch," Dorothy questioned her with one eyebrow raised, "couldn't you have used your charms to kill the Wicked Witch of the East yourself?"

The Good Witch of the North opened her mouth to speak but stopped. Putting a finger to her cheek, she thought a moment and then said, "I suppose I could have. However, I'm a good witch and if I killed another witch, the mere fact of killing her, wicked or not, strips me of my good witch standing. You do see the dilemma?"

"I think I do," Dorothy replied, a bit doubtful.

The Good Witch of the North gave her a broad smile, and added, "However, you're not hampered by such silly restrictions. Since killing the Wicked Witch of the East will not blemish your reputation as a simple-minded little girl, you're free to kill all the wicked witches you want. Congratulations." She reached forward, took Dorothy's hand in her own, and shook it.

"Thank you," responded Dorothy, pulling her hand away and staring at it. "I'm happy to be of service anytime if killing witches is always this easy." She rubbed her hand hard up and down over her dress as though to rid it of some contamination.

"Some things come easier for some than others," the Good Witch of the North winked.

Dorothy scrunched up her face, thinking. "This good witch, bad witch thing confuses me because I thought all witches were bad."

"That's a misconception." The Good Witch of the North took a precautionary step back away from Dorothy. "In case you have it in mind to kill another witch while you're roaming about Oz, you must keep in mind that there are good witches and then there are bad witches. I'm one of the good ones. You won't forget that, will you?" She then pointed to herself and mouthed the words silently, "Me, good witch," while her smile and bright eyes revealed a hint of trepidation.

"Oz? You said Oz. What's that?"

"This is the Land of Oz. It's where you, your house, and your hairy rat landed, deary."

Rat? I growled at the insult. If I didn't know it would displease Dorothy, I would have bitten the Good Witch of the North's ankle for spite.

Dorothy asked, "Speaking of witches, how many are there in Oz?"

"We have or had four witches until now. The good ones are north and south. Do remember that," she emphasized. "The wicked ones are east and west." She frowned a moment and muttered under her breath, "Although, I don't know who will replace the witch of the east. I don't suppose Oz can get along with one area void of a witch, good or bad." She shrugged with a gleeful smile, waving her hands around and around, and my head spun in circles as my eyes followed the stick. "Oh, well, I'm sure this will be resolved in due course. For now, we will just have to get along with two good witches and that awful, dreadful Wicked Witch of the West."

Dorothy frowned, "I will take you at your word that you are a witch, but my Aunt Em told me there are no real witches in the world."

"What part of the world are you from?"

"Kansas."

"Never heard of it." The Good Witch of the North raised her hands high and my eyes shot up in expectation, but then they fell to her sides without letting go of that darn stick. "Then again, I only know the Land of Oz and nothing beyond it."

"You don't get out much, do you?"

"If no witches live beyond Oz why should I? One likes to stay with one's kind."

"I see your point. We don't have witches in Kansas. I mean not real ones. Just a few cranky old ladies I call witches."

"Kansas must be a civilized country if you have no real witches."

"I wouldn't exactly call Kansas civilized," said Dorothy. "It's just... there."

The Good Witch of the North held the stick very still and I lost interest in it for the moment. "With our variety of witches, sorceresses, magicians, and wizards you'll find Oz is not one bit civilized." Offhandedly, she added, "Come to think about it, Oz is a rather odd place." Then, pressing the stick to her breast, she added a cheerful sigh, "Still, to us it's home."

"You have wizards, too?"

"Why? Are you in need of one?"

"Don't know exactly. Though, if I ever did, where would I find one?"

"Well, to be truthful, we have only one Wizard. He is the Magnificent Wizard of Oz. Presumptuous title, but we've gotten used to it."

Suddenly the crowd of Munchkins cheered and pointed. As we turned and watched, the legs and feet of this Wicked Witch of the East shriveled up and disappeared beneath the house, leaving only her sparkly shoes behind.

"What happened?" asked Dorothy, astonished at the sight.

"The old witch dried up like a raisin in the sun," the Good Witch of the North answered, rather smugly I thought. "Those shoes left behind are now your property, my dear." She reached down, picked up the shoes, and shook off what was left of the Wicked Witch from them. Handing them to Dorothy, she said, "One size fits all. Here, take them."

Dorothy grimaced. "Not my style." Then, shrugging, she said, "Still, I might get something for them at a pawn shop when I get home." She daintily carried the shoes by her fingertips into the house. The Good Witch of the North turned to the Munchkins behind her and shrugged her shoulders. After Dorothy placed the sparkly shoes on the table, she came back out.

"It's been nice meeting you, but it's time Toto and I got home."

The Good Witch of the North pointed behind us. "But your home is right there. A very curious, but effective mode of transportation, I may add."

Dorothy sighed and said, "I meant home to Kansas. Can you point me in the right direction?"

"Heavens, no," the Good Witch of the North cackled merrily. "If I never heard of it how can I point you and your furball in the proper direction? Anyway, all I know, all any of us know, is there are vast deserts that lay beyond the Land of Oz to the north, east, south, and west. Possibly Kansas is one way or the other. Then again, maybe not. If you can't find your way I'm afraid you're stuck here forever."

Dorothy placed her hands to her face and burst into uncontrollable sobs. I immediately turned to her and licked her ankles, trying my best to comfort her.

The flood of tears streaming from Dorothy's eyes made all the Munchkins put handkerchiefs to their eyes, and they sobbed and blew their noses noisily with her.

"I want to go home to Kansas," Dorothy sobbed.

The Good Witch of the North rolled her eyes. "Why would you want to do that? You just got here. Stick around and have some fun." She gave Dorothy a playful punch in the shoulder with her fist and Dorothy burst into tears again. The Good Witch of the North scrunched up her face, placed her hands on her hips, and complained, "Come on. I didn't hit you that hard."

"I want to go home," cried Dorothy. "Home to Kansas," she emphasized with a dainty stomp of her foot, just missing my forepaw.

The Good Witch of the North raised her arms and then dropped them hard against her side again while, to my disappointment, maintaining a tight grip on the stick. "Ay Carumba. Let me see what I can do before you flood the place."

"Okay," Dorothy beamed. Her grief and tears magically disappeared in an instant.

The Good Witch of the North eyed her suspiciously. "Taken acting lessons, have you?"

"I don't understand?" Dorothy replied with innocent perkiness.

The Good Witch of the North frowned, then shrugged it off. Taking off her pointy hat, she held it in one hand and used the other to twirl her stick over it. My head spun around and around as my eyes never left that stick. Then my head jerked to a sudden stop when the stick halted. With a poof, the hat turned into some sort of reading board.

"Let's see what it says here." The Good Witch of the North skimmed the board, nodded, and then said, "Yup. It's Emerald City for you girl. Most certainly the Magnificent Wizard of Oz can help you."

"Is he a good or a bad wizard?

"Never met the Wizard personally, but I've heard he tends to be on the good side."

"How do I find this Emerald City?"

"It is at the heart of the land and all yellow brick roads lead to it," said the Good Witch of the North. "You can't miss it. However, I should warn you that the Land of Oz is a dangerous place at times. Though you do have this diminutive creature of yours to protect you." She gave me a dubious look. I perceived a contradiction in the manner and tone of her voice, but I was not about to give it much weight.

Dorothy looked down at me and then back at the Good Witch of the North. "I could use a bit more protection if you get my drift."

Added insurance could only help, I agreed with a wag of my tail.

"Would you like a charm?"

"What kind of charm?"

"A charm for protection."

"Whatever you can drum up."

The Good Witch of the North motioned with her hand. "Bend your head toward me." When Dorothy tilted her head, the Good Witch of the North gave her a big, wet smack of her lips on her forehead, leaving behind a shiny round mark. "There, that should do it. Now I'm off. I have a whole lot of good witch things to take care of. Busy, busy, busy!"

The Good Witch of the North twirled in a rapid circle and, for a moment, faded from view. However, her disappearing act did not go as planned since she rematerialized just as suddenly. She rocked and swayed unsteadily, her eyes rolling in circles in their sockets. She put her hand to the side of her head and said, "Whew. That was a quick round trip. Maybe I need to do it a bit slower so I can stay put once I get to where I'm going."

The Good Witch of the North twirled again, but much slower this time, and soon vanished into thin air for good.

I snapped and growled after the witch while Dorothy reached out and felt around the spot she vacated. She shrugged and said, "I expected she would have used a broom for transportation, but that may only occur in fairy tales and not in real life like this. Right, Toto?"

I barked in agreement, even though I had doubts about the reality of any of this. However, as a human's best friend, it's not my place to question my human companion.

With both witches gone, although one more literally than the other, the Munchkins bowed and began to walk off back into the trees, humming a catchy tune.

ROAD OF YELLOW BRICKS

"Yellow brick road," Dorothy murmured, looking down at the brick pavement we stood on. "Oh well, off we go, Toto. To follow the yellow brick road. To follow the yellow brick road," she repeated as she skipped away down the path, leaving me behind.

I sat down and sized up the situation. She seemed a bit too nonchalant, I thought, venturing nearly alone in this unknown land, but that was Dorothy's nature. Forever trusting those she meets. Since my sole occupation is safeguarding Dorothy, I observed her with a keen eye, trying to determine what I could do to ensure her well-being on what could prove to be a perilous journey. It is then that I noticed her shoes appeared a bit worn. I looked back into the house and saw the Wicked Witch's shoes on the table. They looked to be in very good condition, so I dashed in and leaped on a chair and onto the table, but before I retrieved the sparkly shoes, I noticed a small wicker basket with a handle next to them. Sniffing, I realized there were loaves of fresh bread beneath the argyle-patterned cloth. Knowing we might get hungry along the way, I picked up each shoe and placed them on top of the cloth, then took the handle of the basket in my mouth and hopped back down. Trotting off after Dorothy, I stopped a moment to sniff a tree and relieve myself. Satisfied, I grabbed the basket again and took off after Dorothy.

I caught up with Dorothy and then ran ahead a few feet. There I stopped, turned, put the basket down in front of Dorothy, and barked my thoughts regarding the sparkly shoes.

Dorothy knelt and patted me on the head, pleased with my thoughtfulness. However, when she picked up the sparkly shoes she appeared as though she was about to cast them off into the bushes, but, reconsidering, she looked them over carefully.

"I wouldn't be caught dead wearing these in Kansas," she grumbled. "A little too flashy for my taste, but we're not in Kansas, are we?" I barked in agreement. "Although used, they are in better condition than my shoes." With that, she kicked off her worn shoes and replaced them with the sparkly shoes. Then she stood, rocked back on her heels, and said, "A surprisingly good fit."

I trotted beside Dorothy, my little feet working furiously to keep up with her as she skipped along, her sparkly shoes tinkling almost musically on the hard surface.

We were off to Emerald City in a land that the Good Witch of the North described as dangerous. Who knows what perils lurked ahead of us? Even if we reach Emerald City and locate this wizard, there was no guarantee he would help us return to Kansas. Still, it amazed me how Dorothy took all this in stride. Given that I was there to protect her, you could see why she maintained such confidence.

IT WAS NOT LONG BEFORE we came across a beautiful and multi-toned countryside where bountiful fields of grain and vegetables stretched far into the horizon. Little houses with domed roofs and fences lined these fields.

Dorothy pointed and said, "Look, Toto, everything is painted blue. The houses, fences, and even the people standing in the doorways are dressed in blue. They must be Munchkins, too."

From their doorways, Munchkins bowed and cheered as we passed by. They must have heard we were the slayers of the Wicked Witch of the East and looked upon us as heroes.

Toward evening, growing tired, we slowed our pace and wondered where we were to stay the night, but soon we came upon a house larger than the rest. Out on the neat little lawn, fiddlers played and men and women danced while others laughed and sang merry tunes. Near them, fruit, nuts, pies, cakes, and other treats sat on a large table. Sniffing the air, my mouth watered and my tail wagged with excitement. I looked up and saw Dorothy running her tongue over her lips before she smacked them. If she had a tail, I am sure it too would have wagged.

The owner of the house, Bog, invited us to join the feast.

As we joined the festivities, it was I, not Dorothy, that drew the most attention for Munchkins had never seen a dog. Children delighted in chasing me and pulling my tail and I did my best to resist snapping at them and biting their little fingers off out of respect for our host. That and the fact that Dorothy took great pleasure watching me with the children.

Bog, glancing at Dorothy's sparkly shoes, remarked, "You are a sorceress of prominence."

"Why do you say that," responded Dorothy.

"You killed the Wicked Witch and wear her shoes and your frock is white."

Dorothy looked at her dress, smoothed it out a little, and replied nonchalantly, "My dress is checked white and blue."

"Only witches and sorceresses wear white, and blue is the Munchkin color, therefore you are a great and good witch."

"Whatever. Though, I'd just as soon that you think of me simply as the little girl that I am," she replied in her typical modest pose.

"Still, you must be very brave for we feared the wicked witch you so effortlessly murdered."

Dorothy blew a breath on the fingernails of one hand and polished them on her blouse. "It was nothing, really."

At evening's end, our host provided us with a place to sleep, and in the morning, after a hearty breakfast, Dorothy asked Bog, "How far is it to Emerald City from here?"

Bog gave a grave warning. "I have never been there, but I know it takes many days, some of it traveling through very dangerous regions. You'd be wise not to go unless you have important business with the Great Wizard."

Dorothy frowned, somewhat worried, but replied, mustering courage, "It is the Wizard of Oz, I am told, who can help me return to Kansas."

"Is Kansas more beautiful and bountiful than here?"

Dorothy grimaced. "Well... not exactly. Dusty, drab, flat, and mostly gray and you would be hard-pressed to find a decent place to get a meal. Still," she sighed, her shoulders rising and dropping as though they weighed a ton, "it's home."

"To each, his own," shrugged Bog.

"Well...?" Dorothy, reconsidering for a moment, appeared indecisive.

I wagged my tail, my mouth open, and my tongue quivering with excitement, hoping she would abandon her desire to return to Kansas. The Land of Oz, so far, seemed pretty neat to me and I got more attention there than I did in Kansas, but alas, to my dismay, she was determined to go on.

SCARECROW

Bog wished us well and, refreshed and replenished with bread, cakes, and pie, we again took off on the yellow brick road. We had traveled several miles when Dorothy stopped to rest on top of a fence that bordered yet another vast field. I saw her head turn to something behind her and I ran under the fence to see what drew her attention. There, propped on a pole high above the stalks of corn was a man. An unusual-looking man and I kept a cautious eye on him as I crept toward him, my nose up in the air sniffing suspiciously.

"It's not a real man, Toto," Dorothy explained with a chuckle. "I know it looks like a real man because it has a Munchkin's hat, clothes, and boots, but it's only stuffed with straw. Even its head is nothing more than a burlap sack with a face painted on it. Someone hung it on that pole to scare crows away so they call it a scarecrow."

I sat down directly below it, studied, and appraised its construction when, all of a sudden, its eye closed and opened in rapid succession. Startled, I barked furiously, backing away.

"What is it, Toto?" Dorothy asked and then gasped, "Oh my! It winked."

The scarecrow had tilted its head toward Dorothy and it flashed the same eye to her.

"Oh my," remarked Dorothy, aghast.

I barked and barked. Then the scarecrow's head flopped over the opposite way, and a painted smile spread across its painted face. It was taunting me and that infuriated me even more. I growled, sprang, and snapped my teeth at its boot, but the boot was too high for me to get a good bite of it.

"Stop that, Toto," Dorothy said. She slid off the fence and took one slow step after another toward the scarecrow. The scarecrow's head flopped over the opposite way and this time smiled at Dorothy.

"Hello there," its painted face said in a friendly manner.

Dorothy stopped in her tracks and pressed a hand hard to her cheek. "You... you spoke!"

"So I did," it confessed, its eyes bright and cheery. "How are you this day?"

"Fine, thank you," Dorothy curtsied, cautious not to take her eyes off the scarecrow. "And yourself?" she asked after a moment's hesitation.

Scarecrow sighed, "Not very well, I'm afraid. For you see I am stuck on this pole day and night with little to do but shoo crows away. An occupation I am not very good at." Just then, a crow landed on its shoulder. Scarecrow tried its best to shake it off and said, in a feeble manner, "Shoo, shoo," but the crow was disrespectful of his efforts and ignored him. "See what I mean? If only I could get down from this pole I would be much happier." It sighed again.

"Well..." said Dorothy, looking to me for advice. I growled my uncertainty, but Dorothy said, "It is made of straw. What harm could it do?"

I could not argue with that and I watched as she walked behind Scarecrow, whisked the crow away with her hand, and then, after a few ladylike grunts, she lifted Scarecrow off the pole and dropped him to its feet where he wobbled precariously weak-kneed in circles, yet managed to stay upright. I backed away growling and barking, but Dorothy stepped right up to it and took it by the shoulders, steadying it.

"Thank you." The Scarecrow bowed at the waist but nearly fell over in its attempt. Regaining its balance, it said, "It has been a while, but I should get the hang of standing and walking shortly."

"You talk and you stand and walk," Dorothy observed correctly, although somewhat puzzled.

"Not bad for someone without a brain," Scarecrow replied with moderate pride. "If only..." it put a stuffed gloved finger to its burlap head, "...I had brains I could do much more than hang on a pole day and night, night and day. I could think and ponder and wonder and dream and possibly come to conclusions."

"Although," Dorothy warned, "I would not be too quick to conclude. Conclusions are not always correct."

"If I had a brain I would realize that," Scarecrow let out a heavy sigh. Then, looking into the basket Dorothy held at her side, he said, twirling a stuffed gloved finger over it, "I don't suppose...?"

Dorothy pulled back the cloth and showed him the contents of her basket. "Just bread and a bit of cake and pie. No brains, I'm afraid."

"Whatever should I do?" Scarecrow tried to ponder the thought, but he lacked the brains to do so.

An idea came to mind and I barked with eagerness, "Why not let Scarecrow come with us and see if the Great Wizard can find brains to give him?"

"Toto, no!" Dorothy stomped her foot. She either disagreed with my proposal or somehow misinterpreted what I said, something she often did. To Scarecrow, she said, "Do not be afraid, Toto will not bite you."

"What is there to be afraid of?" he stated with confidence. "I'm made of straw. You can stick a pitchfork into me and it will go right through and I would hardly notice." He stuck his leg out to me and said, "Go ahead, bite if you will."

I obliged by clamping onto a mouthful of straw between the boot and pant leg and yanking it away.

"Toto, stop," said Dorothy, bending and taking hold of my mouthful of straw. She pulled and tugged, but I would not let it go so easily. However, I soon grew tired of the game and gave up the struggle.

Dorothy, kneeling, stuffed the straw back beneath his pant leg. "It may not harm you, but if you thought about it you'd know you need all the straw you can handle to support you. There," she said and stood again.

"If I had a brain I'm sure that thought would have come to me."

With that, I ran back under the fence and sat in the middle of the yellow brick road. I barked, restating my suggestion, and this time I knew Dorothy understood me because she turned to Scarecrow and offered my suggestion.

"We are on our way to the Emerald City to ask the Wizard of Oz if he can help us get back to Kansas. Possibly, being a Great Wizard, he might be able to find a brain for you."

"Give me a moment to think this over." Scarecrow stood back, put a finger onto his chin, and tapped it slowly. A very, very long moment went by before he threw his arms up in frustration and said, "Nil! Zilch! Zero! I am at a loss for a qualified reason to dispute, quarrel, contest, or oppose your offer. My head is a complete blank."

"You certainly do need a brain," Dorothy responded with a sigh. "Although, I know real people in Kansas who have brains and can't do much better than you in the thinking department. Politicians, mostly."

I barked, "Someone without a brain would be a good fit in Congress, considering all the brainless Congressmen that generally occupy it," but neither the Scarecrow nor Dorothy appeared to be listening to me.

"Come," Dorothy started for the fence, squeezed between the railing, and stood on the opposite side, waiting.

"You don't mind if I join you?" asked Scarecrow.

"Even if you don't get brains," said Dorothy, "you can come in handy when I need a soft place to sleep. I can yank all the stuffing out of you to make a nice bed and use your empty clothing as blankets."

"I could be useful at that," agreed Scarecrow. He walked in a cocky manner toward the fence, ran right into it, and flipped, head over heels, to the other side. Without missing a beat, Scarecrow bound to his feet and brushed himself off as though nothing had happened.

"See, not a scratch. You will be grateful to have me along because I can stand between you and any danger we might encounter."

"To do what exactly?" asked Dorothy.

"I will stand firm and do nothing. Well, as firm as a man of straw can stand."

"That's your plan? Do nothing?" Dorothy glanced at me and rolled her eyes.

"You see, the danger will be so busy ripping me apart and scattering me to the wind that it will give you time to run away," explained Scarecrow.

Dorothy thought a moment. "Could work," she said, buying into it.

"However, once the danger has left the scene, I would appreciate it if you could return and restore me to my former self."

"That would depend on how far we ran away," said Dorothy. "Still, I will consider it. That's if I'm certain the danger is not lurking about in the shadows, waiting for our return."

IT WAS ABOUT NOON WHEN we stopped to rest and have a bite to eat. Dorothy broke off small pieces of bread and spread it on the ground for me and then tore off a chunk, and offered it to Scarecrow.

"No thank you," Scarecrow said, smiling. Pointing to his painted mouth, he added, "Nowhere to put it. Also, if I did have a hole in my mouth the bread would simply get clogged up in my straw."

"I see," said Dorothy, munching on a piece of bread. "At least you don't have to stop and find a place to relieve yourself afterward."

"Relieve me of what?"

"Little clumps of bread with a straw stuck to it, I guess," shrugged Dorothy.

It was not a pleasant subject at mealtime and I was happy Scarecrow changed the subject.

Scarecrow sat drumming his fingers on his thighs, gazing about. "Is Kansas a more beautiful place than here?" he asked.

"Not exactly," said Dorothy. "It's dark, dusty, flat, and gray. It has very few trees or flowers and is filled with dull, drab people."

"Then why do you want to return?"

"You're not very bright, are you?"

He pointed to his head, smiling. "Empty nest."

"If you had brains you'd understand that people, real people with brains in their heads, would rather live in a dark, dusty, flat, and drab place if it is where they came from."

"I see," he replied, nodding his empty head. He raised a finger and surmised mindlessly, "It takes brains to stay away from beautiful places such as we have here or else Kansas would be vacant as my head."

"No place like home," Dorothy assured him with a heartfelt sigh. "There just isn't."

I opened my mouth to bark in agreement, but the more I thought about what Scarecrow said the more it confused me, so I let the subject drop.

TIN WOODMAN

After a short rest, we headed off again in good spirits, but as the hours passed, the yellow brick road began to decline and our spirits diminished with it. I soon found myself having to leap over holes or uprooted bricks while Dorothy walked around them. Scarecrow, though, took no heed of the rough conditions and stumbled, tripped over, or fell into whatever lay in his path. This seemed not at all to bother him. Each time Dorothy hoisted him back to his feet, he would laugh it off and continue to the next mishap without a care in the world.

Along with the decaying road, the countryside grew bleak. The fields were rutted, uncultivated, and without fences. The few farms and houses we saw were in disrepair and untidy, as well as the Munchkins who occupied them. No one waved or smiled. They just stood in doorways with a look of gloom on their faces.

As we continued, the road of yellow bricks led us into a dense forest of intertwining branches that blocked the light from reaching the ground, making it difficult to see. Not having much choice, we continued to follow the road of yellow bricks until it faded below the branch and leaf-littered ground. Knowing this road must reappear on the other side somewhere, we ventured on undaunted.

As evening came, we chanced upon an empty cottage and decided to spend the night. Dorothy and I slept on a bed of leaves in one corner while Scarecrow, never tiring, stood in the opposite corner with nothing to do but wait for dawn. I was sure the time passed quickly for him for, without brains, he could not grasp the passage of time. This ability, or lack thereof, could be an advantage in the daily and nightly duties of scarecrows and night watchmen alike.

IN THE MORNING, AFTER a simple breakfast of bread and water, the three of us set off again. This part of the forest was not as dense as before and allowed some light to penetrate. Enough light for us to locate traces of a road of yellow bricks below the debris that covered the forest floor.

While we walked, Dorothy asked, "Please tell me a story to while the time away."

I thought she was speaking to me and I barked my story out with enthusiasm.

"See, it's about this little girl and her magnificent and brave dog and they get caught up in this great wind that whirled them off into a faraway and strange land..."

I didn't get very far into my story before Dorothy hushed me. I realized then, she had asked Scarecrow and not me, and he went into some dreary story about a puppet maker named Geppetto, who stitched Scarecrow together, painted his face, and brought him to life. Then, when he ventured off into the world to seek his fortune, a farmer kidnapped him. The farmer propped him on a pole in the middle of the cornfield to scare crows away. Even though this appeared to be the end of his story, Scarecrow continued to talk. What more could there be for the life of a scarecrow besides hanging on a pole in a field day and night, night and day? Having lost all interest, plus having a short attention span, I decided to take myself for a walk and do a little sniffing about.

I had not gotten very far before my nose got a whiff of something peculiar. At about the same time, I heard a deep, long groan. I stopped in my tracks, looked deeper into the woods, and spied a shiny man with an ax oddly frozen in place as he was about to whack a tree. Near him were pyramid displays of stumps of trees that looked to be the result of his previous mutilations and, no doubt he was about to add another to the pile. Infuriated with the damage to beautiful and useful trees (I, like any other dog, seldom can go far without needing one) I lunged at him with the intent to inflict pain. My jaws widened and my fangs clamped into his ankle with a loud, metallic, hollow clunk! Stunned and with teeth aching and head swimming, I staggered backward and tried to recompose myself. What was this man made of, I wondered? Once recovered, I looked at his very round, shiny leg, but I could not find evidence of my assault. However, my assault must have had some effect for I heard him moan and groan again, more deeply than before. Seeing that I could do little to stop this perpetrator without assistance, I decided to put my scent on him and mark him for future reference.

"No, Toto," Dorothy cried out just as I lifted my leg to his ankle. "That is so rude!" she added with a little stomp of her foot.

Submitting to her command, I painfully forced myself to cease and desist further action.

Speaking to Dorothy, Scarecrow advised thoughtlessly, "It may also dull or stain the lustrous sheen of this fine craftsmanship."

The shiny man groaned again and Dorothy took a cautious step to get a closer look. "You groaned?"

"Indeed I have," moaned the shiny man despondently through a clenched mouth. "You see, it has been more than a year since the rains came, rusting me in this exact position, unable to move an inch more."

Scarecrow ambled up to the shiny man and looked him over. "From his posture and with a raised ax, it appears his occupation is that of a woodman." He rapped his gloved knuckles on the shiny man's side and his straw-filled hands produced a soft, hollow sound. "It also appears he is wrapped in a thin layer of tin, yet, from the audible response I received, he lacks any substantial structure within. A hollow tin man. However, if I may suggest, that if his maker had substituted aluminum for tin he may not have found himself in this..."

Tin Woodman groaned, "Oh, shut up and do something to help me."

"Yes, but what, Tin Woodman?" Dorothy asked.

"In my cottage down the road, you'll find a can of oil."

Scarecrow asked, "Can you point us in the proper direction?"

"If I could move to do so I would not need oil," grumbled Tin Woodman. "Besides, it is the only cottage within miles of this forest. You may have passed it."

"Yes, of course," said Dorothy. "We had spent the night there."

"Oh, that cottage," said Scarecrow. "If I had a brain to think with I'm sure it would have occurred to me that the cottage must belong to a woodman for we are in the woods and here you are, ax in hand with a pile of wood beside you."

"You do a lot of talking for a man with a face painted on a burlap sack," grumbled Tin Woodman irritably. "Please shut your painted trap and get my stinking oilcan!"

Thinking quickly and without any command, I darted back in the direction of the cottage. Once inside, I sniffed around. Besides the leaf bed, the only other objects in the cottage I could see from my vantage point was a wooden stool by a small wooden table, but my nose told me that something lay hidden from view on the table. Leaping upon the stool and then onto the table I found a shiny half-domed object with a long narrow stem protruding upward from its center. Sniffing, I surmised this foul-smelling object must contain the oil Tin Woodman requested. Disregarding its unpleasant taste, I clutched its stem with my teeth and dashed back to the others.

Taking hold of the oilcan, Dorothy applied it to the joints of Tin Woodman, freeing one extremity after another. Flexing his arms, legs, and neck, they made a grinding noise at first until each moved without hindrance or creaks.

"Ah, this is so much better," Tin Woodman thanked Dorothy. He lowered his ax and bent to pat me on the head. I growled tentatively at first but submitted and accepted this gesture as condolence for the harm he had inflicted on trees. Ascertaining that as a Woodman, he has little choice, but to chop wood.

"Not many come through these woods," Tin Woodman said. "May I ask your destination?"

"Emerald City," replied Dorothy.

"What is your purpose there?"

"To seek the Great Wizard so that he may help me get back to Kansas."

"The Wizard of Oz is a great wizard I am told," said Tin Woodman. "Do you think he can find a heart for me?"

"I don't see why not."

"That is a modest request, considering your shortage of required viscera," agreed Scarecrow, again tapping Tin Woodman's round chest with his gloved hand and producing a reverberating hollow echo. "Empty shell."

"Even with the required viscera or internal organs to be exact, without a heart, I'll still be a shell of a man," sighed Tin Woodman.

"Then join us," said Dorothy.

Of Dorothy, Tin Woodman asked, "If you would, please keep the oilcan in your basket for I may need it if I find myself caught in another drenching rain and rust up again."

"Certainly," replied Dorothy. She added, "Are you familiar with the ins and outs of this forest? The road of yellow bricks is not always clearly visible."

"Certainly," said Tin Woodman, resting his ax over his shoulder. "I know the way with, or without the help of the yellow brick road."

With that, the four of us headed off to Emerald City.

When we reached a large hole in the path, I sprang across it while Dorothy and Tin Woodman walked around it. Scarecrow, however, took no heed of it and fell right in. Tin Woodman picked him up and Scarecrow marched right ahead without thanking him since it would have been a repetitive gesture considering the many times Scarecrow continued to fall or stumble.

"Why didn't you walk around the hole?" inquired Tin Woodman after about the fifth time.

Scarecrow, ambling along, replied, pointing to his head, "No brains. When I am full of them things will be much better."

"Brains are overrated. All one needs is a heart."

"Why do you want a heart?" asked Dorothy.

"Well, you see," Tin Woodman's face attempted to look forlorn, but being rigid, it fell short. "I was not always made of tin or even hollow. I was once a full-bodied human such as you. Though not as dainty."

Scarecrow looked Tin Woodman up and down. "I should hope not."

"What happened to change you into a woodman made of tin?" asked Dorothy, covering up a yawn with her hand.

"The Wicked Witch caused it all," Tin Woodman sighed. "It began when I met this beautiful young Munchkin girl and I asked her to marry me. She said she would once I earned enough money to build us a home. With this incentive, I went off into the woods and worked harder than ever before. To my misfortune, the Munchkin girl lived with this very lazy old woman. The old woman wanted the Munchkin girl to stay forever with her, cooking, cleaning, and taking care of her."

Scarecrow yawned, his painted mouth wide open, even though he had no breath to inhale or exhale.

"To this end," continued Tin Woodman, "the old woman approached the Wicked Witch..."

"Of the east or west?" asked Scarecrow.

"East, I think."

"You don't have to worry about her anymore," said Scarecrow. "Dorothy bumped her off only yesterday."

"It was an accident, I assure you," said Dorothy. "Toto and I were in a house that fell from the sky, smashing the Witch."

"You couldn't steer the house away from the Witch?" asked Scarecrow.

"It seemed to have a mind of its own," responded Dorothy.

"There you have it! Scarecrow complained bitterly. "A house with a brain and me... nada!"

Tin Woodman cut in, "Can I get back to my story?"

"What story?" Scarecrow asked.

"Yes, please do," said Dorothy.

Tin Woodman let out a huge sigh. "Promising her livestock and a few random children, the woman asked the Witch to do something to block our marriage. The Wicked Witch agreed and, the next day, while I was out chopping wood, she bewitched my arms, directing them to swing the ax down and chop off a leg..."

"Right or left?" Scarecrow requested a clarification.

"Right. This, of course, left my career as a Woodman in doubt. Undaunted, I approached our town's tinsmith and asked for his help, and soon I was back at work with a tin leg. The Wicked Witch, not wanting to be outdone, reappeared and beguiled my arms again to chop off my other leg..."

"Left?"

"Left. Again, I returned to the tinsmith who then fastened another leg of tin, but, holding to her promise to the old woman, the Wicked Witch would not give up. She then bewitched one arm to whack off the other."

"Right or left?"

"Right. I returned to the tinsmith who hammered out a tin arm replacement that included a working tin hand and affixed it to my shoulder."

"Next, you're going to tell us the Wicked Witch made you chop off your left arm," Dorothy surmised.

"How did you guess?"

"You can skip to the next part," Dorothy sighed. "Since we already know about your arms."

Tin Woodman agreed and went on. "Now with two tin arms and legs, I again worked furiously, but the ol' Wicked Witch forced my tin hands to swing the ax at my neck, chopping off my head. One would think this would be the end of me, certainly."

"We would assume so ruff-ruff," Dorothy, Scarecrow, and I chimed in chorus. "But we would be wrong ruff-ruff, since you're here ruff-ruff, telling us the story ruff-ruff."

Tin Woodman nodded his tin head in agreement. "Fortunately, the tinsmith arrived on the scene and found my tin body lying there and my head nowhere in sight. Being a clever tinsmith, in no time at all, he constructed a tin head to fasten to my body and helped me to my feet. So back to work I went, working even harder than before with tin arms, legs, and head, but still with a human torso. Then the Wicked Witch struck the final blow. Moving my tin arms, she made the sharp ax turn and slice my human torso completely in half."

"One would think you would then be a goner for sure ruff-ruff-ruff-ruff-ruff," Dorothy and I replied jointly, astonished.

"One would think," agreed Tin Woodman.

"Not me," said Scarecrow, pointing to his straw-filled head. "I never think at all."

Tin Woodman ignored him. "But this is Oz, after all."

"After all of what?" asked Scarecrow.

Tin Woodman narrowed his eyes and he would have grimaced if he could. "However the tinsmith rescued me again, assembling a body made of tin to attach to my other tin components. This, though, left me hollow, and without a heart. With no heart, I lost all desire for the Munchkin girl I loved and I have remained alone in the woods chopping wood."

Scarecrow put a finger to the side of his head a moment, and then asked, "Is it your belief that if you had a heart your love for this Munchkin girl would return and you would marry her?"

Tin Woodman nodded forlornly in agreement. "Without a heart, there is no love."

"Are you sure you wouldn't rather have brains?" asked Scarecrow. "Brains can come in very handy, I am told."

"The Wicked Witch has brains, and look what she has done to me," answered Tin Woodman, showing his irritation with the Wicked Witch. "Although, if she had a heart, she would have refused the old woman and allowed us to marry and be happy."

"If I had any brains I would have concluded that," Scarecrow muttered in an airheaded manner.

Dorothy, to my surprise, simply shrugged her indifference to the subject and said, "Brains, heart, whatever. What is most important is that Toto and I get back to Kansas as soon as possible. All this chatter is slowing us down. Let's hit the road, Jack." Hooking the basket in the crook of one arm, she picked up her pace and skipped off.

"Well, I am off to see the Wizard," Dorothy chimed merrily.

"The Wonderful Wizard of Oz?" asked Scarecrow, scurrying on unsteady legs to catch up to her.

Tin Woodman, remaining behind, called after them. "Because…?"

"Of the wonderful things he does," Dorothy responded.

"Oh," said Tin Woodman.

Scarecrow swung his arm in circles, beckoning Tin Woodman to join them.

Tin Woodman, with another quick flexing of his joints, took off after them in a lumbering, squeaking trot.

I sat back on my haunches. With my head tilted to one side, tongue hanging out, and wagging my tail, I stared at them from behind. What a curious trio they made. If I didn't know any better, I would think I was dreaming all this up, but since I don't have an ounce of imagination, I knew this had to be real. Still, I sat a moment longer wondering if our little adventure could get any more peculiar. When I heard Dorothy's shrill whistle, it broke me from my short contemplative moment and I dashed off after them without a thought of what might lie ahead of us.

LION

As we continued, the forest became denser, casting dark shadows over us. Here and there, we spotted the sections of yellow road under forest debris and felt we were going in the right direction. Then, in the distance, we began to hear deep-throated growls.

"Tigers?" whimpered Tin Woodman.

"Lions!" Scarecrow worried.

"Or bears," I barked, though not at all intimidated.

"Oh my," said Dorothy, a little frightened.

We slowed our pace, looking cautiously this way and that way, fearful that something may be behind a large tree or a thick bush. Tin Woodman held his ax high and I gritted my teeth, snarling, ready to strike at anything that sprang from the darkness of the woods.

Suddenly, a horrific roar stopped us in our tracks, and out from behind a large tree, a menacing lion jumped in our path. Scarecrow spun his arms in circles and advanced on him, prepared to pound him with his gloved fists, but the lion, with a swipe of his great paw, sent him flying backward over our heads.

Before Tin Woodman could raise his ax, the lion struck his chest with his claws, knocking him flat on his back.

It was my turn and I took one meaningful step after the other until I was inches from his massive form. I stiffened, gritted my teeth, and growled threateningly, ready to pounce. The lion looked down and around trying to locate his adversary. Then, after a long moment, he spotted me directly below him and he opened his jaws wide. I looked unflinchingly into his cavernous mouth filled with long, razor-sharp teeth and, as he roared, I held my ground and stiffened even stiffer against the blast of his hot, smelly breath. When he finished, he closed his mouth and gazed down at me again with a look of bewilderment at finding me still there. Undaunted, I leaned back on my haunches and snarled, ready at any moment to leap and clamp my teeth onto his furry leg, when, all of a sudden...!

SMACK!

"Ouch! That hurt!" cried the lion.

It was a good thing for the lion that Dorothy stepped in and slapped him on the nose, or else I would have gnawed his hide until he squeaked for mercy.

"What did you do that for?" asked the lion. Stupefied, he rubbed his paw delicately over its nose.

"You could have swallowed him whole," grumbled Dorothy with a little stomp of her foot. "Only cowards pick on such small, defenseless creatures." I resented Dorothy's depiction of me as defenseless, but I knew she meant well.

The lion appeared to melt, humbly and sadly, under her glaring stare. Then, looking again at me, the lion asked, "Exactly what is that... that thing?"

"A meat-eating dog," said Dorthy

"Do you cut his meat for him?" wondered the lion

"Don't change the subject," Dorothy wagged her finger. "Why do you do such cowardly things like picking on creatures much smaller than yourself? You are the King of Beasts, and as the King of Beasts, it is your duty to grapple with creatures much bigger and stronger than you are. Even though they can rip you apart, tear you to shreds, eat your heart out, and drink your blood."

"I'd like to see you step into my shoes and see how you like it," the lion challenged, though timidly.

"I would if I could, but you don't wear any, shoes I mean."

"Sure, take the easy way out." The lion rolled his eyes.

"You're getting away from the point," Dorothy stomped her foot again.

"Look, I admit I'm a coward. I'm even afraid of little things," the lion pointed a paw at me, "even things as small as that toad."

I barked, "I'm a dog," correcting him.

The lion flinched and quivered. "See? I'm shaking."

"Oh my," said Tin Woodman from his reclining position behind us.

The lion, wiping a tear with the tip of his tail, sniffled, "I am a coward, a cowardly lion."

"However, you roared and attacked us," said Dorothy. "You did not appear afraid of us."

"I panicked," the lion confessed.

"I would hate to see you get angry," Scarecrow's muffled voice cried out. We looked back and saw him on the ground twisted into a pretzel shape. "You nearly knocked the stuffing out of me. Ah, I could use a little help here," he added.

"I can still hear ringing in my ears," said Tin Woodman.

Dorothy walked back to Scarecrow, untwisted him, and stood him on his feet, and together they aided Tin Woodman to a standing, yet tilted position.

"Normally my roar scares everyone and they run away, but none of you did," whimpered the lion. "If creatures of the woods knew that I would be too frightened to fight back if they stood up to me, even itty bitty things, I wouldn't last long. To protect myself, I hide my cowardliness behind the reputation that lions are the feared Kings of Beasts. That, and the fact that I'm a good size for my age, and I have a tremendous roar."

"You're a fake," said Scarecrow, adjusting and stuffing straw back into the vital portions of his body and head.

Lion nodded with a despondent sigh. "It makes me sad to live without courage and to live in fear of all around me. My heart pounds rapidly when danger is near."

"Heart disease," suggested Tin Woodman.

"You think so?" the lion asked, with hopeful wide eyes.

"You're lucky to have a heart that can become diseased," lamented Tin Woodman. "I have no heart, therefore I can never have heart disease."

"If I had no heart, I might not be so cowardly," said the Lion.

"How about brains?" Scarecrow asked. "Do you have brains?"

Lion felt his head with his paw and rolled his eyes toward his forehead. "I suppose so. I've never looked inside."

"Brains are things you might want to consider if you have the brains to consider it with," suggested Scarecrow. "That is why I'm going to Emerald City, to ask the Great Wizard of Oz if he can provide me with brains."

"I'm going there to ask the Great Wizard if he can find it in his heart to spare me a heart," said Tin Woodman.

"I'm going there to ask if he can find the means to return me to Kansas," added Dorothy.

"Ruff!" I said, not wanting to remain silent about my part in all of this.

"Do you think the Great Wizard of Oz has the courage to give me?"

Scarecrow opened his painted mouth to answer but held back a moment. Then he put a finger to the side of his head and scrunched up his face. "Are you asking if is possible that the Great Wizard has the courage within himself to provide you with courage or are just hoping he might have some extra courage sitting about in the courage department that he can afford to offer you if he can summon the courage to do so?"

Not bothering to comment, we set off again to the Emerald City.

THE LION, WHOSE NAME happened to be Lion, strode stately on one side of Dorothy and I on the other. At first, I did not think too highly of Lion. After all, he did threaten to take a bite out of me or swallow me whole. Though as fierce and intimidating as he appeared, I knew Dorothy would always rely on me for comfort and protection. Therefore, I decided to let bygones be bygones and we got along just fine from then on.

It was not long before Tin Woodman led us out of the forest and into a valley where the yellow brick road was easily visible once more. By then, it was dusk and we settled at the edge of a large tree farm for the night.

Dorothy dug into her basket and pulled out a small piece of bread. "Toto, this is all, I'm afraid." She broke the bread in half and shared it with me. "We will go hungry if we do not find more food."

Lion spoke up quickly. "I know humans prefer cooked meat so I will go into the forest and hunt down a deer and kill it so you may cook its meat over a fire."

"Oh dear, no!" Tin Woodman gasped. "I do not wish you to kill a deer to eat or for any reason. If you harm a living creature, I will grow very sad and it will make me cry and I fear my tears will flow and rust my jaw shut."

"Then I will not kill a deer," said Lion.

"Nuts," Dorothy grumbled.

"Yes, nuts," Scarecrow agreed. He looked at the tree farm. "I believe those are almond trees. I will collect the nuts for you, Toto, and Lion to eat."

"None for me," Lion thanked Scarecrow. "I'm not a vegetarian."

"So what will you do?" asked Dorothy.

Lion looked far beyond the trees to the other side of the farmland and spotted a light in the window of a distant farmhouse.

"Humm," Lion muttered under his breath. "If you will excuse me, I think I'll do a little exploring." With that, he wandered off through the field of almond trees to fend for his supper.

Scarecrow went about collecting nuts. Wanting to help, and a bit famished, I took Dorothy's basket between my teeth and followed Scarecrow around. Although Scarecrow tried his best, his padded gloved hands made the effort of gathering nuts difficult, and most of what he picked slipped and dropped onto the ground, but, eventually, he managed to fill the basket.

It was getting chilly, so Dorothy asked Tin Woodman if he would chop down a small tree for firewood. She then stacked the wood in a pile and, showing some ingenuity, rubbed two sticks together and managed to start a fire without a match.

I sat next to Dorothy near the fire and she cracked nuts and fed some to me. However, Scarecrow stayed clear of the fire for fear a spark would set his straw ablaze. It did not matter to Tin Woodman where he sat as long as his tin body did not overheat.

It was not long before Lion returned, smacking his great lips and feeling revitalized. He did not say what he fed on and we did not want to know. However, feeling something caught between his teeth, Lion rubbed his great tongue over them, then turned his head to the side and spat out a pointy blue hat.

DEEP RAVINE

At dawn, Dorothy awoke and washed in a nearby brook before we set off again. We had not traveled more than an hour when the yellow brick road ended abruptly at a wide and deep ravine.

"Oh my, what shall we do?" asked Dorothy. "The sides are too steep to climb down or up and there are sharp rocks at the bottom if we fall into it."

Scarecrow looked at the ravine and considered it. "I give up," he said, throwing his hands into the air. "Let's go back." He turned and started on his own, back the way we came.

Lion, however, gauged the width of the ravine and said, "I think I can leap across it."

"What about us?" asked Dorothy.

Scarecrow, hearing this, spun around and came back. "I have it," he said, rejoining us. "We can each take turns on Lion's back and ride over to the other side. I will go first. If the distance is too great for Lion and we fall, landing on those sharp rocks below it will not harm me for I am made of straw."

"What about me?" Lion asked. "There are meat and bones under this hide."

"Yes, what about you?" asked Tin Woodman. "A coward would not attempt such a dangerous maneuver and it is a coward you claim to be."

"I am a coward," Lion insisted, with a long, sad sigh. "Still, I see no choice. If I want to reach Emerald City so that I can ask the Great Wizard to give me courage, I must do it. Hop on Scarecrow, you're going for a ride."

Scarecrow climbed on Lion's back and wrapped his arms around his neck for security. Lion then walked to the edge and crouched back on his haunches.

"Aren't you going to back up and take a run at it?" asked Scarecrow.

"I'm of the cat family," said Lion. "Cats leap." With that, Lion sprang across the ravine and landed Scarecrow safely on the other side. Lion then turned and sprang back over. With me in her basket, Dorothy climbed up on Lion's back and we flew through the air. Once Lion brought Tin Woodman over, we returned to the yellow brick road.

KALIDAHS

The road of yellow bricks led us into a narrow valley. On one side were low rolling hills and, from the other side, we began to hear strange noises.

"Kalidahs," warned Lion.

"What are Kalidahs?" Dorothy asked, not at all liking the sound of it.

"Beasts with the bodies of bears and the heads of tigers," explained Lion. "They are huge and walk on two legs like a human."

"Or like a Scarecrow," Scarecrow added.

"Or like a Tin Woodman," Tin Woodman dittoed.

"Bark-bark!" I raised my front paws in the air and walked on my hind legs to demonstrate how the Kalidahs walked in the event Dorothy still did not grasp the concept, but she paid no attention to me.

As the sounds of the Kalidahs seemed to get nearer, we picked up our pace but, as luck would have it, we came to another wide and deep ravine much wider and deeper than the ravine we crossed before.

Lion shook his head sadly. "I'm sorry, but I cannot leap that distance."

Scarecrow, surmising the situation, noticed a large tree at the edge of the ravine not far from us. He then turned to Tin Woodman and asked, "Why don't you chop that tree down so it will fall over to the other side of the ravine? We can then cross it one at a time."

To me, Scarecrow seems very clever for someone without brains. Though having a short attention span, this thought quickly faded from my mind.

As Tin Woodman hacked away at that tree, I got a scent of something coming our way and barked the alarm.

Seeing two Kalidahs charging from between two small hills, Dorothy cried, "Oh my! I am so frightened that my heart pounds."

"I wish I had a heart so it may beat rapidly," said Tin Woodman, hacking away. "Just heartless, that's what I am, but who cares?"

Whack! Whack! Whack! Whack!

Scarecrow felt around his chest but had no idea where one kept a heart. "If I had brains, I would know where to look for it," he muttered to himself.

Lion turned on the charging Kalidahs and roared, stopping them in their tracks. "That was easy enough," he said, surprised by his accomplishment.

The Kalidahs, not as big as Lion, took a moment to confer. Once they realized they outnumbered him two to one, they charged once again.

"Oops," said Lion, now very much afraid.

The tree then fell to the other side of the ravine and all of us scooted across its trunk one after another. Although we made it safely to the other side, the beasts had reached the tree and were making their way across it toward us.

"Quick, Tin Woodman," said Scarecrow, "chop the top of the fallen tree in half so it will fall into the ravine, taking the Kalidahs with it."

Tin Woodman swung his ax and hacked away. The hacked portion soon broke and the Kalidahs fell, growling horribly to their demise.

Thump! Augh!

Thump! Augh!

Then, no more.

Dorothy, looking down over the edge of the ravine at the two Kalidahs splattered on the rocks below, slapped her hands across one another as though brushing them off. "Good. Didn't like the looks of them anyway," she said in a carefree manner.

We did not know why the Kalidahs were after us, nor did we give any thought to their brutal, bloody demise. Instead, we returned to the yellow brick road and continued merrily on to our destination.

STORK

We soon came to the edge of a broad, swiftly flowing river. Our side of the river was lined with succulent fruit trees. On the other side was a beautiful meadow with budding flowers. However, we saw no way to get from one side to the other.

Scarecrow, looking down at the road of yellow bricks that abruptly ended at the edge of the river bank and reappeared on the other side, complained, "Who in their right mind would build a yellow brick road ending at broad ravines and rivers without the means of going across any of them? Very short-sighted and mindless they must be."

"Possibly a troupe of scarecrows paved the way," suggested Tin Woodman.

"This would account for the shortsightedness," agreed Lion. He tapped the side of his head with his paw. "No brains."

With his hands on his hips, Scarecrow frowned. He appeared poised to dispute their theories but he lacked the brains to argue the point that this could not have been the result of the stupidity of scarecrows. Nor did he have the brains to feel offended by this generalization. Instead, he shrugged and walked away without a thought in his head.

Tin Woodman and Lion looked askance at each other. "Scarecrows," they assured each other with a nod of their heads.

"Oh my," said Dorothy, flopping on her bottom on the grass. "How shall we ever cross?"

Scarecrow, Tin Woodman, and Lion flopped too.

"Whatever shall we do?" they bemoaned sorrowfully.

I, of course, did not take our predicament sitting down. I looked around and spotted some twigs on the ground and then, looking back at a small grove of trees, a thought came to mind. I quickly gathered the twigs in my mouth, trotted to the edge of the river, and piled them neatly on the ground. Turning back to my companions, I barked my idea to them, but no one stirred or bothered to look my way.

"Ruff-ruff-ruff," I repeated, but much louder this time. However, it was only Scarecrow who paid attention to me. He stood and walked over, leaving the others behind.

To demonstrate what I had in mind, in case Scarecrow had not grasped what I had barked, I gathered up the twigs again and dropped them in a pile into the river. Then I snatched a small nut and flung it out toward the twigs. The nut landed exactly where I wanted it to, in the middle of the pile of floating twigs.

Watching the tiny raft float away, Scarecrow scratched his burlap head, shrugged, and then sauntered back to the others. Stupefied as to why my idea of constructing a raft to carry us across was not workable, I flopped on the bank of the river, my head resting on my paws, and brooded forlornly. Then, moments later, Scarecrow hopped up to his feet and did a little dance, his painted mouth smiling brightly.

"A raft," he said, excitedly. "Tin Woodman can chop trees and build a raft to cross us to the other side."

"That is a wonderful suggestion," Dorothy, Tin Woodman, and Lion applauded Scarecrow, patting him on the back and nearly knocking him over. As always, they overlooked the originator of the idea, but I suppose that's the life of a dog. Especially one that is as diminutive as I am and easily overlooked by just about everyone.

Even though Tin Woodman set off to hack away right away, it took time to cut enough wood to build a raft big enough to carry us all. Still, he worked tirelessly long into the night to complete the job. In the meantime, Dorothy wandered the banks of the river and collected fruit from the trees to add to our meal of nuts. Once Dorothy had her fill she fell asleep and I snuggled up next to her, licking at my paws.

At sunrise, Dorothy and I woke to find Tin Woodman fastening the logs together with the help of Lion. Scarecrow, with his burlap hands, could do little to help, except to offer mindless advice that Tin Woodman and Lion ignored.

After Dorothy washed at the edge of the river, she gathered more fruit and together we feasted on a light breakfast and waited until the raft was completed. Once Tin Woodman and Lion pushed the raft onto the water, we all boarded.

Dorothy sat in the middle and I jumped up into her lap. When Lion stood in one corner, the raft tilted, but Scarecrow and Tin Woodman hurried to the opposite corner to balance it. With long poles, Scarecrow and Tin Woodman dug down deep into the mud below and pushed us across. Unfortunately, the river deepened toward the middle, and their long poles could no longer dig down into the mud and were useless. Without the aid of the long poles, the fast-moving current drove us downstream, and we watched as the yellow brick road began to fade from view behind us.

"We are heading toward the land of the Wicked Witch of the West," bemoaned Lion. "She will cast spells on us and make us her slaves."

"Then I will not get my brains," bemoaned Scarecrow.

"Or my heart," whimpered Tin Woodman.

"No courage for me," Lion grumbled.

"I will not find my way back to Kansas," sighed Dorothy.

"Ruff-ruff," said I, offering encouragement in these distressing times. I could tell they appreciated it since they all smiled sadly at me and Dorothy patted my head and rubbed my back.

As the rushing river moved us closer to the opposite bank, Scarecrow looked down into the water and said, "I think it's shallow enough now to use my pole and take control of this raft." He immediately rammed his pole down, but, to his misfortune, the pole stuck in the mud with Scarecrow holding fast to it, while the raft continued downstream without him. Hanging onto the pole barely above water and looking quite bewildered, Scarecrow waved goodbye to us.

"Stuck on a pole again, but over water instead of a cornfield," Dorothy lamented. "Oh, what will he do?"

Made only of straw and clothing, I knew he did not weigh enough to sink and he could easily float downstream and eventually catch up to us. Scarecrow, of course, did not have the brains to figure this out on his own, so I barked loudly, "Let go of the pole and drop into the water." Scarecrow was too far away to hear me and my suggestion was all for naught.

"We are less a pole and I fear if I attempt what Scarecrow did," Tin Woodman worried, "I too will get stuck on a pole and all I could do is watch the rest of you go downstream without a paddle." He began to cry, but fearing he will rust, he took the cloth from Dorothy's basket and wiped his tears away.

I looked at the bank on the other side and judged its distance and the swiftness of the river. Although I was not very large, I knew I must attempt to save everyone. Taking hold of the end of Lion's tail between my teeth, I jumped into the water and began to dog-paddle the raft to the bank. However, I had barely taken a stroke before Lion lifted his tail with me hanging onto it and deposited me back onto the raft.

As I shook the water from my body, splashing everyone, Lion said, "I think I can swim to shore while pulling the raft. Before I jump in, take hold of my tail, and hang on."

I barked at Lion, "What do you think I was trying to do before you pulled me out?"

"Hush, Toto," said Dorothy, drying Tin Woodman before he rusted. Then, together, Dorothy and Tin Woodman grabbed hold of Lion's tail. As Lion dove into the water, I latched my teeth onto the knot of Dorothy's apron at the small of her back, keeping everyone on the raft as Lion swam to the shore. When we neared the bank, Dorothy took command of the pole and pushed us the rest of the way to the shore. With a final push and a ladylike grunt, Dorothy grounded the raft on the bank and we all jumped off, a little bit exhausted, but relieved.

Lion trotted off a good distance away from Tin Woodman to shake the water from his body. When he returned, Dorothy said, "Now that we are on the opposite side of the river we need to return to the road of yellow bricks if we want to reach the Emerald City."

"Then we need to follow the bank back up the river," said Lion.

Once refreshed, we ventured up the river bank until we got sight of Scarecrow. While he held on for dear life to the pole, a smug-looking crow perched on his shoulder, and then pecked at his straw and dropped it into the water.

Dorothy frowned. "How are we going to get Scarecrow from that pole and onto the shore?"

Just then, a large stork flew over our heads carrying something in a cloth bundle with his beak. Circling, the stork swooped down and landed near us. He gently placed his bundle down on the grassy bank, eyed it a moment, and then turned to us. He wore a little white cap on his head and, with his broad wing, he raised it and tipped it toward us and said, "Excuse me for the intrusion. My name is Stork, and I need direction."

Tin Woodman quickly stepped forward. "The Lord giveth and the Lord taketh away," he offered devotedly, pressing his ax to his chest where one normally keeps a heart.

"Not that kind of direction," Stork frowned. "Direction to a cottage of a young couple that is expecting."

Tin Woodman thought a moment, then shrugged. "In that case, you're out of luck."

Stork turned back to the bundle and appeared to be leaving when Dorothy approached him and asked, "Even though we can't help you, could you possibly help us? It should only take a moment of your time."

Stork looked at each of us, and asked, "Who are you?"

"I'm Dorothy and these are my friends; one cowardly Lion, a heartless Tin Woodman, and oh, that's my brainless friend, Scarecrow, who you can see is stuck on the pole in the middle of the river."

"Your friends have distinctive characterizations," said Stork. Then, looking down at me, he asked rather arrogantly, "So what trait do you designate to this odd thing at your feet?"

I didn't much care for the tone of Stork's question and I growled softly.

"Toto? He's just a dog if that is what you mean."

"A dullard," Stork replied pompously.

I tilted my head to one side and looked up at him, not quite sure what he meant by that.

Stork asked, "So, how can I be of assistance?"

"If you would kindly fly over the river and carry our friend, Scarecrow, back to us we will be very grateful."

Stork's bundle moved a bit and he eyed it closely until it settled again. Then, looking over at Scarecrow, he said, "He is quite large and may be too heavy for me to carry."

"Ruff," I differed.

"No, he is only made of straw and very light," said Dorothy, agreeing with my assessment.

"Well," Stork pushed his little cap back on his head with his wing and said, "I will try, but if he is too heavy I will have to drop him into the river."

"Ruff," was my response, unable to shrug my shoulders.

"Watch my bundle, please," Stork said. "Don't let your lion or your diminutive fur ball companion get at it. It is quite valuable to the receiving party and they will be very upset if it came to them chewed or with parts missing."

I raised my snout and sniffed the air from where I sat. Lion raised his snout, too, and sniffed and I was certain he took in the same sweet, powdery fragrance that I did for he slowly ran his great tongue over his massive lips. He was about to smack his lips when Stork jerked his head and eyed him sternly. Lion simply turned his eyes skyward and whistled innocently.

"Be assured no one will touch your bundle," Dorothy said, frowning at Lion. "You have my word on it."

Lion continued to whistle.

With a nod to Dorothy, Stork flapped his powerful wings and soared over to Scarecrow. When he lowered his large talons, the crow on Scarecrow's shoulders grew fearful and flew away. Taking hold of Scarecrow, Stork easily lifted him and carried him over to us.

"Thank you so much," said Dorothy after Stork dropped Scarecrow in a heap onto the shore.

"Glad to have been of service," replied Stork. "Since you are unable to offer me direction, I must hurry and seek it elsewhere."

"Not so fast." Scarecrow leaped to his feet and offered, "Naked came I out of my mother's womb, and naked shall I return thither." He gave a nod to Stork. "How's that for starters?"

"Won't do any good," Tin Woodman sighed, shaking his head sadly. "A nonbeliever."

"Very sad indeed," said Scarecrow. "One must find their way, I suppose."

Stork, his beak open to respond, snapped it shut and shook his head, confused. "I better be on my way. Delivery times are not set in stone, but expectant mothers do worry when their bundle is overdue."

Then, grabbing the tied end of the bundle with his beak, he flew off.

THE BIG SLEEP

Reunited, we started back toward the yellow brick road; which led us into the fields of beautiful flowers of various kinds. Birds flew overhead chirping gaily and we all thought it was a wonderful place to be.

"Oh, I love the smell of these flowers," said Dorothy, breathing deeply.

I sniffed and sniffed, and had to agree with her. They were of an unusual scent, quite fragrant and pleasing to the senses. Although, the farther we walked, one large flower in particular, dominated the others until the field of flowers was only of this one kind.

"I'm feeling sleepy," said Dorothy, slowing her pace. "The scent of these flowers is overpowering."

I sniffed and snorted, sniffed and snorted, and I too felt a little dazed and tired. I soon could not walk in a straight line and staggered sideways.

"Oh, I feel so sleepy and tired, too," said Lion, staggering much like me.

"What are these flowers?" asked Tin Woodman.

"Scarlet poppies, I believe they are called," said Scarecrow.

"Scarlet poppies?" Tin Woodman appeared alarmed. "I have been warned of the aroma of these flowers before I was built entirely of tin. They can be overwhelmingly intoxicating and will certainly put you to sleep."

"I feel just fine," said Scarecrow, doing a little dance to demonstrate. "I don't feel tired at all."

"Not you, stupid," said Tin Woodman. "We are not made of flesh and blood and the aroma does not affect us, but look at the others."

Dorothy stopped and sat down and I fell over to one side. She closed her eyes and was soon snoring. I looked through droopy eyes at Lion and saw him plop down, unable to go on.

"Yikes!" said Scarecrow. "So what does this mean?"

The last thing I heard before falling fast asleep was Tin Woodman explaining, "It means if they fall asleep here amid these toxic poppies the aroma will cause them to sleep forever and they will eventually die." Not a pleasant thought to hear as one retires.

SQUEAK! SQUEAK! SQUEAK!

These shrill noises woke me from my slumber, but still dazed, it took me a moment to realize we were out of the poppy fields and surrounded by mice. Overjoyed that I was alive, I barked with glee and bounded into their midst, but they scattered horrified in all directions, and disappeared into the grass.

Tin Woodman swooped me up into his arms and called out, "Queen of Mice, please return. I will not let Toto harm you. You and your subjects will all be safe."

I wagged my tail, panting. Harm them? Absurd. I only wanted to introduce myself and, if they were willing, engage them in a game of chase to loosen the kinks in my body after sleeping so soundly.

Then a stately-looking mouse, dressed in a long, flowing gown, with a crown on its head and carrying a scepter in its hand appeared apprehensively and asked in almost a whisper. "Are you certain the great beast will not eat us?"

I felt an itch on my tongue and it took several swipes on Tin Woodman's tin cheek before it subsided.

"See," said Tin Woodman, "he is as harmless as a mouse."

The Queen turned to the other mice and said, "We must abide by the woodman's word, for he has saved me from the Wildcat."

"It was merely a swing of my ax that saved your Queen," said Tin Woodman in all modesty. His ax, resting over one shoulder, dripped with blood. "Since I have no heart, I have to try harder to protect defenseless creatures such as yourself from great harm."

"In gratitude, we must do your bidding," said the Queen.

It was then that I noticed a large, hairy creature lying on the grass. It lay in two parts, its head sliced cleanly from its body. A gruesome sight to me, but one that drew little attention from the others. I also saw Dorothy nearby. She was sound asleep in a sitting position, snoring loudly, unperturbed by the commotion around her.

"How, then, can we repay you?" the Queen asked Tin Woodman.

Tin Woodman thought a long moment and then said. "I have no idea."

Scarecrow, who had been standing by silently, placed a finger to the side of his head and said, "We are missing a friend. He remains in the poppy field fast asleep. We must retrieve him or he will surely die. Since he is of considerable size and weight, we'll need a large cart to carry him back here. To that end, Tin Woodman can start by chopping down some trees by the river's edge and then sculpting them into boards, pegs, and wheels from which we will construct our cart. Once this is completed, we will harness as many mice as we can to pull it."

There was a long moment of silence as we all stared in disbelief at Scarecrow's well-thought-out proposal.

Scarecrow tapped the heel of one hand against the side of his head a few times. "If I had a brain, it would be hurting about now."

The Queen turned to Tin Woodman and asked, "Who is this friend in need of our help?"

"Lion," answered Tin Woodman.

"Squeak!" the mice cried out all at once. "A lion! He will eat us all in one bite."

"He's a cowardly lion and will not harm a soul," Tin Woodman assured them.

"Okey-doke," all the mice said, appearing satisfied.

After working furiously, Tin Woodman and Scarecrow completed the cart. Once they harnessed the multitude of mice the Queen had summoned to the cart, Tin Woodman and Scarecrow led them into the poppy field. With Dorothy fast asleep, I stayed behind to keep her company.

When they returned with the sleeping Lion in the cart, Tin Woodman and Scarecrow removed the harnesses from the mice; which took a long time since there were so many of them. Then the mice gathered around Dorothy and I. It was only then that Dorothy's eyes opened and she looked about.

"Eek! Mice!" Dorothy cried out, startled. She jumped to her feet and hopped onto the cart where Lion lay sleeping. Dorothy took hold of the hem of her dress and raised it above her knees. "Eek! Eek! Eek!" she cried again.

"The nervous type," the Queen said to Tin Woodman.

"Let me introduce you," said Tin Woodman. "Dorothy, this is Queen of Mice and Queen, this is our friend Dorothy."

Dorothy let go of her hem and rubbed her eyes as she shook off a yawn. She looked again at the mice. She frowned a moment and then curtsied. "Pleasure to meet you, Your Highness." She yawned again. "You'll have to excuse me, but I just woke up from a deep sleep and forgot where I was."

The Queen turned to Tin Woodman and said, "We must go now. If you are ever in need of our assistance again, just give a little whistle. Tweet-tweet."

"Give a little whistle, tweet-tweet," repeated Tin Woodman.

"Give a little whistle, tweet-tweet," all the mice squeaked.

I tried to purse my lips to whistle, but dog lips don't purse.

Lion woke in time to see the mice depart and asked, "What's going on?"

"It was like this," Tin Woodman began. "You, Dorothy, and Toto had fallen asleep in the fields of poppies, but Scarecrow and I are immune to the fragrance because we cannot smell and we do not sleep. Scarecrow and I then carried Dorothy and Toto out, but you were too big for us to rescue and we found it necessary to leave you behind. When I saw the Wildcat chasing the Queen, I swung my ax and chopped off its head, killing it. In gratitude, the Queen offered to help us. The idea of constructing a cart to carry you came about and, when the cart was completed, we managed to lift you onto it and brought you here."

"Mice, you say," said Lion.

"Mice," said Scarecrow. "That's the plural of a mouse. Their queen, Queen, is the one with the little crown and flowing gown."

Lion eyed them closely. "Appetizing to look at, but not a fulfilling meal, I'd imagine."

"I promised that you would not eat them," said Tin Woodman.

Lion frowned.

"Enough chit-chat," Dorothy interceded, eager to get back on course. "We must hurry and reach Emerald City before some other misfortune derails us."

GATE GUARDIAN

Back on the yellow brick road, we left the fields of flowers behind, crossed over a small hill, and came into a valley with neat little cottages with fences.

"This is much like the Munchkins' homes we stopped at before," said Dorothy. "Only here everything is painted emerald green. Even the people in doorways watching us pass are wearing emerald-colored clothing with pointed emerald-green hats. Since everything here is emerald green, we must be near the Emerald City."

Anxious to get to Emerald City, we continued until late afternoon. By then, still feeling the effects of our time in the field of poppies, Dorothy, Lion, and I grew drowsy again.

Dorothy suggested, "Why don't we ask the occupants of that nearby farm if we could stay the night and have something to eat."

The occupants were kind enough to feed and bed us, and when we told them that we were on our way to see the Great Wizard of Oz, they informed us that, although the Great Wizard will surely grant each of our wishes they could not guarantee that we would meet him face to face. He was so reclusive that not even his servants knew what he looked like. When he did appear, it was always in some exotic form such as a bird or fairy, but never as his true self, whatever that true form was. Given that he is a Great Wizard, and wizards are mostly likely courageous, brilliant, generous to a fault, and the best companion one could ever wish for, I concluded that his true form most certainly is a breed of dog. A Cairn terrier, perhaps? Having ascertained this knowledge by deduction I more than ever wanted to meet the Great Wizard Dog!

THE NEXT MORNING, REFRESHED after a good night's rest, we again took to the yellow brick road and it was later that afternoon when we noticed the horizon glowing ahead of us.

"The sky is glowing green so the Emerald City must be just over that ridge," said Dorothy. "Let's hurry before night falls."

Reaching a great wall embedded with sparkly emeralds, Scarecrow waddled up to its main gate and knocked with his gloved fists in repeated succession. However, with a hand stuffed with straw and covered with burlap, it was too soft to make a sound. Still, that did not deter Scarecrow from impatiently rapping his fists soundlessly even though no one from the inside responded.

"We know you're in there," fumed Scarecrow. "Why don't you let us in?"

It was obvious to me that no one within the gated wall heard the soft tap of Scarecrow's knock, but it did not seem so obvious to the others as they waited in line behind him. I would have suggested that Dorothy attempt a knock, but her fists were too dainty to produce much of a sound. Lion's paw was huge, but much like my own paw it was soft and furry and he would do little more than claw a tap. I thought our best chance would come if Tin Woodman clanked with his tin fists or his ax. However, as I gazed about, I noticed a big button next to the gate. Realizing it was there for a purpose, I ran up to the wall below it and barked my discovery until I got everyone's attention.

Dorothy, Tin Woodman, and Lion came up behind me. Dorothy, gazing at the button asked, "I wonder what this button is for. Maybe I should push it."

Scarecrow, continuously rapping his fists soundlessly, said, "If the occupants of this city can't hear my knock how can they hear the sound of a button being pushed?"

"Possibly," suggested Tin Woodman. "The act of pushing the button will produce a sound within the wall."

"If it is connected to a bell or electrically wired," agreed Lion.

They studied the button intensely and all appeared to agree that the button had some useful design yet they could not decide what to do with it. Growing impatient, I clawed at the wall and barked, "Just push the doggone button." I don't know if anyone was listening to me because it took a long while before Dorothy gave in to my request, put the tip of her finger to the button, and pushed. Suddenly, behind the great wall, a bell tingled and the gate swung open.

Grouped closely together, we entered a high-arched room where we found a little man dressed from his hat to his shoes all in emerald green. Next to him was a very large emerald green box.

"Are you the Great Wizard?" asked Dorothy.

"Heavens to Betsy, no," replied the little man. "I am Gate Guardian. Guardian of this gate. What can I do for you?"

"We are here to see the Great Wizard on business," replied Dorothy, standing firm and resolute.

"Well, you can blow me over with a breath," said Gate Guardian. We each drew in our breaths and blew hard, sending Gate Guardian promptly backward onto the seat of his pants. Tin Woodman and Scarecrow helped him back up on his feet. "It has been a very long time since anyone has come to see the Great Wizard," he explained, brushing off the seat of his pants. "It is not a foolish or mindless business you seek of him, is it? For, if it is, the Great Wizard will surely annihilate you."

"Got a temper, has he?" asked Scarecrow.

"No," said Dorothy, "it is very important business."

"As guardian of the gate, I must take you to him." He then turned to the emerald green box. After producing a key from his pants pocket, he unlocked it. "First, you must wear glasses that I will lock onto your heads. This will prevent the brilliance of the Emerald City from damaging your eyes."

"We all have to wear them?" asked Scarecrow. "My eyes are only painted on."

"My eyes are made of tin rivets," added Tin Woodman.

"That does not matter. Even this lion and the squat creature beside him must wear them," answered Gate Guardian. "It is by order of the Great Wizard of Oz that all, even those who live within the city, must wear them at all times for you'll see the city is so glorious and bright that it will blind you."

Gate Guardian, selecting pairs of glasses of various sizes, passed them around for us to try on. After Scarecrow and Tin Woodman donned theirs, they helped Lion with his. Lion's glasses were enormous and in comparison, the glasses Dorothy fitted on me were tiny. All the glasses had chains that went around to the back of our heads with little locks attached to them. Gate Guardian reached into the big box and took out a smaller box. Opening the smaller box, he produced a second, smaller key and used it to lock the glasses. From his pocket, Gate Guardian took out a pair of glasses and locked them on his own head. When he had finished, Gate Guardian put the smaller key back into the smaller box and placed it back in the big emerald green box. Utilizing the first key, he locked the big box and then put this key in his pants pocket.

"There is only one key for all the glasses in the Emerald City," he said, patting the pocket with the key, "and I retain the only key to open the box to retrieve the box with the key to unlock the glasses."

"Job security," Scarecrow deduced.

"Also a tongue twister," Tin Woodman noted.

Turning to another great door, Gate Guardian took a large key from a peg on the wall next to it and unlocked it. Lo and behold, even though we wore the glasses, the brilliance of the inner city dazzled us all as we entered.

EMERALD CITY

"Look, Toto," said Dorothy, in wonderment, "such beautiful houses built of emerald green marble, and studded with sparkly emeralds."

"The road is also made of emerald green marble," added Scarecrow, in awe, "with each block edged with shiny emeralds."

"Even the glass of the windows is green," remarked Tin Woodman.

Lion looked up. "The sky has a green tint to it, too."

As we passed by, mothers and their children stopped whatever they were doing to watch us.

"Strange," said Dorothy. "Everyone is dressed in green, and they even have a green tint to their skin."

Lion, looking them over, smacked his lips. "A refreshing aromatic mint green."

Mothers, noticing Lion eyeing their children, hurriedly rushed them indoors.

"Everything everywhere is brilliantly green," I barked, and then added, "Though all this green is a bit extreme if you ask me."

As we followed the Gate Guardian, I noticed everyone was staring at me as we walked by. Then I realized that there were no dogs to be seen anywhere in the Emerald City and it made me sad to think that no one had a dog to comfort, entertain or protect them. Even though they lacked the companionship of dogs, they tried their best to project a sense of happiness and contentment, masking their misery and loneliness.

We soon arrived at a large building which Gate Guardian said was the Palace of the Great Wizard and he walked up to a soldier stationed at its great door.

Gate Guardian addressed the soldier as Soldier and announced, "This odd assortment of organisms and things would like an audience with the Great Wizard." He specified us in a pleasant, but official manner.

"We don't need an audience to see the Great Wizard," corrected Scarecrow. "I would think we can see him quite nicely all by ourselves. If I could. Think, that is."

Dorothy turned to Soldier and said, "Yes, we want to see the Great Wizard badly, and be quick about it!"

Soldier snapped to attention and waved his hand toward the door. "Please enter and I will immediately go to the Great Wizard and announce you."

We followed Soldier into a great emerald green hall.

"Please wait while I go to the Throne Room," said Soldier.

"Couldn't he wait until he sees the Wizard before going to the bathroom?" asked Tin Woodman.

Scarecrow replied, "I would speculate that Soldier was referring to a room housing a great chair that is generally reserved for someone of importance, such as the Great Wizard, and the chair in it is generally referred to as a throne. However, since I am brainless I would not place much faith in this hypothesis."

"You certainly could use a brain," said Tin Woodman with a sympathetic sigh.

It was a very long time before Soldier returned.

Dorothy jumped to her feet excitedly from where she had been sitting on the floor and asked, "Did you see the Great Wizard?"

Soldier shook his head. "No one has ever actually seen the Great Wizard. Still, I did speak to him and he said he would grant you an audience." Soldier jerked his head to look at Scarecrow, but this time he remained silent. Turning back to Dorothy, he continued, "However, only one of you can enter each day." Counting each of us, he added, "This means it will take several days before all of you have your turn to speak to him. Therefore, I will provide rooms for each of you." He pulled out an enormous whistle and blew on it and the shrill sound brought a young girl scurrying at once. "This is Girl and she will show you to your rooms."

With a bow, Girl said to Dorothy, "This way, please."

Dorothy picked me up, waved goodbye to the rest, and then scurried after Girl who was hurrying down the hall. Girl led us this way and that way and then up some stairs to a room overlooking the front of the Palace. The room was very beautiful and comfortable and it had a fountain in the middle of it that sprayed sweet-smelling water up into the air. While I sniffed the water, Dorothy tried on several lovely dresses from the closet that fit her perfectly, as though made for her. Then she took a little book from a bookshelf and flopped herself onto a soft, velvet-covered bed, and began to laugh as she thumbed through the book.

Unable to thumb anything and, with nothing to do other than sit and watch Dorothy lay on the bed, I decided to follow Girl as she returned to the others.

One by one, she led each to their rooms in various parts of the Palace, and, each one, just like Dorothy's, was splendid. Though the rooms were as comfortable as Dorothy's, Scarecrow, unable to close his painted eyes, did nothing more than stand just inside the door, staring continuously at a spider weaving a web up in the corner of the ceiling. Tin Woodman, out of habit from the days he was flesh and blood, lay on his bed, but he did not sleep or even try to rest. Instead, he continually exercised his arms and leg joints to keep them flexible. Lion, however, acted more naturally, springing up onto the bed and curling into a ball. After a few seconds, he purred himself to sleep like an ordinary cat.

MAGNIFICENT AND MALICIOUS

In the morning, Girl returned. "Would you like to wear this satin dress?" she asked, taking the dress out of the closet and presenting it to Dorothy.

"It is a beautiful green satin dress," replied Dorothy, trying it on.

"This satin green apron will go well with it," Girl suggested.

After Dorothy slipped the apron on and tied it on her back, she found a ribbon and dangled it in front of me. "This pretty green ribbon will look good on you, Toto," she said, tying it around my neck. "There, we are all set to visit the Great Wizard."

We followed Girl into the hall outside the Throne Room where ladies and gentlemen of the court, all dressed in vibrant costumes, stood about talking amongst themselves. "Even though they come each day and loiter in the hall outside the Throne Room," Girl said, "none had ever seen the Great Wizard personally, and are never permitted to do so."

As Girl led us through the hall to the Throne Room door, one of the ladies gasped and asked, "Do you plan to see the face of the Great Wizard?"

"Why not?" asked Dorothy, a little miffed by the question.

"He will certainly see you," said Soldier who mysteriously appeared before us. "The Great Wizard was reluctant at first. However, when I explained you wore the sparkly shoes that only witches wear, and you have a shiny spot on the middle of your forehead that only another witch can smack with her lips, he agreed."

"Oh," replied Dorothy, having forgotten about her sparkly shoes and the shiny spot the Good Witch of the North smacked on her forehead with a kiss.

I yelped and salivated when I heard a bell ring. Then Girl said, "The Throne Room is open. Please step inside."

Trotting beside Dorothy through a small door, we entered a huge circular room with high-arched walls embedded with emeralds. At the very center of the room, a brilliantly illuminated cluster of emeralds formed a large circle on the floor. The light from it made everything sparkle so vividly that we had to squint even though we wore glasses to protect our eyes. At one edge of the circle was a marble throne with this enormous bald head sitting on top of it. There wasn't a body, arms, or legs. Just a big, bald head with big ears, eyes, nose, and mouth. Spooky, I thought.

The eyes of the enormous head turned and looked at us and its mouth opened. I expected to hear a roar but was surprised when the voice sounded rather ordinary.

"I am the Wizard of Oz," Wizard Head spoke. "Magnificent and Malicious. And you?"

Dorothy curtsied, "I'm Dorothy. Petite and Passive." Then, pointing to me, she added, "This is Toto. Puny and Pungent. Though that could change once I bathe him."

Wizard Head looked at Dorothy a long moment and then down at her sparkly shoes. "Who gave you those shoes?"

"I took them from the Wicked Witch of the East, after my house landed on her, squashing her flat," Dorothy replied in a merry tone.

"You murdered her with your house?" Wizard Head asked in an even voice.

Dorothy put a finger to her lips, thinking. "It was an accident," she replied lightheartedly.

"She is dead, is she not?"

"Stone dead. Crushed, trodden, compressed, and compacted, I'm afraid"

"So you are a murderer," Wizard Head proclaimed without raising his voice.

"I'm just a little girl," maintained Dorothy, scrunching up her face.

"You rode your house down on top of her, killing her, did you not?"

"I could not have easily left the house in midair," Dorothy responded serenely.

"A manslayer," Wizard Head affirmed simply.

"I'm a girl, so that would make me a murderess, not a murderer, and since the Wicked Witch of the East was a woman I cannot be classified as either a slayer of men or a man who slays."

"How many more have you murdered?"

"None." Dorothy appeared offended by the question, but then, offhandedly, she added, "Well, you might say I had a hand in the deaths of two Kalidahs on the way over here."

"That's three dead by your own accord," Wizard Head calculated calmly.

Dorothy counted the fingers on one hand and shrugged modestly. "Although I really can't take full credit for the Kalidahs. My friends helped."

Wizard Head looked at her forehead. "That mark on your head."

Dorothy turned her eyes up toward her forehead. "Oh yes. The Good Witch of the North planted that with a smack of her lips before she sent me off to see you."

"Why did she send you to me?"

"So you can return me to Kansas."

"As punishment for your murderous ways?"

"Because that is where I came from. It is where I live. Kansas is my home."

"Then, if you return, justice will be served," remarked Wizard Head in a soft drone.

Dorothy sighed. Getting to the point of the matter, she demanded, "Will you help me or not?"

"Only if you do something for me."

"Why do I have to do something for you?"

"In the Land of Oz, you don't get something for nothing. It is the law. My law."

"What do you want me to do?"

"Kill the Wicked Witch of the West."

"I'm not a killer," Dorothy argued cheerfully.

"What about the Wicked Witch of the East and the two Kalidahs? You seemed to have an affable nature for murder. Besides, you have already stated you are a murderess."

"If you're so magnificent and malicious, why don't you kill her yourself?"

"I do not have a house to drop on her."

"You think I can repeat that trick?"

"Possibly not, but you have a knack for leaving dead behind you. You might consider using the powerful charm of those sparkly shoes you wear."

"They didn't come with instructions."

"Come, come. I am certain you will find something at your disposal to eradicate the witch."

Dorothy's mood suddenly changed and tears flowed from her eyes. "I don't want to kill anybody," she cried. "At least not on purpose, or Sundays."

"If you want to return to Kansas you will have to do as I have instructed."

"What if I refuse?" Dorothy stomped her little foot, just missing my paw.

"Then have a nice lifetime stay in the Land of Oz," Wizard Head smiled and winked.

Dorothy seemed absolutely bothered by the request to kill the Wicked Witch of the West and she turned and stomped out of the Throne Room, disheartened.

When we got back to our room, she flopped herself on the bed and wept. I sat nearby wagging my tail trying to think of how I could help her, but nothing came to mind. As each day passed, the others returned with their versions of what went on in the Throne Room.

"I did not see a big head at all," said Scarecrow. "What I found was a beautiful woman sitting on the Throne. She told me to kill the Wicked Witch of the West in exchange for a basket full of brains."

"How did ruff you ruff reply ruff?" Dorothy and I asked simultaneously.

"With no brains in my head, I could not think of how to reply so I left and came back here." Scarecrow shrugged.

Next was Tin Woodman's turn, and he found neither a big head nor a beautiful woman, but an enormous rhinoceros with five eyes, five long arms, and five long and slender legs growing out of its body.

"The beast roared and if I had a heart," his voice rose nervously, "it would surely have beaten so hard it would have broken right through my tin body."

Dorothy, Scarecrow, and I harmonized the same question, "Did he ruff ask you ruff to kill the ruff Wicked Witch of the West ruff-ruff-ruff-ruff?"

"It said that I would receive a great big kind heart only if I helped Dorothy kill the Wicked Witch of the West stone dead," Tin Woodman answered sadly. "I don't have the heart to do such a thing even if it means I would get a heart for doing so."

When Lion returned from the Throne Room on the last day, he said, "I was greeted by a giant ball of fire. It was so hot it nearly singed my mane."

Dorothy, Scarecrow, Tin Woodman, and I voiced our question in perfect unison. "What did ruff the ball of flame ruff request of you ruff in return ruff for granting ruff your courage ruff?"

"The same as the rest of you," replied Lion nervously. "It wanted proof that the Wicked Witch of the West is dead at our hands or I will always remain a coward. The ball of flame intensified and got so hot that I left quickly and even then it nearly burnt my tail off."

"What shall we do?" Dorothy sniffled.

"We have no choice, but to find the means to do away with this Wicked Witch," replied Lion.

"I don't think I can kill the old Witch even if means I will never see Aunt Em, Uncle Henry, or Kansas ever again," bemoaned Dorothy.

"Even if we did find the Witch I don't have the brains to figure out how we can go about killing her," Scarecrow sighed despondently.

"I am too heartless to harm anyone," Tin Woodman said, making sure not to let his tears drip and rust his body as he sniffled. "Even a wicked old witch." He wiped a few tears and flicked them away.

"I certainly don't have the courage to attempt it," Lion lamented in a low roar.

If we were to get anywhere, I knew I had to take charge of these timid bleeding-heart mindless cowards and I did not waste any time barking at them, insisting that we get going on the double.

"I think Toto wants to be taken for a walkie," suggested Lion.

I growled fiercely and clamped my teeth onto the cuff of Scarecrow's pant leg, easily pulling him toward the door.

Tin Woodman offered an alternative suggestion. "He's hungry for a meal of straw, no doubt,"

"Dogs don't eat straw," Dorothy corrected him, "and Toto generally takes care of his walkies. He is very self-reliant in that respect."

As I dragged Scarecrow out into the hall, he hopped on one foot, suggesting to the others, "If I had a brain in my head I would say that Toto is trying to tell us something. Possibly that we should prepare by having Dorothy add new paint to my eyes so that I see more clearly and add more straw to bulk up my body. For Tin Woodman to sharpen his ax, and oil his joints. For Lion to rest so that he will be strong and untiring in the morning. Then, once we find and kill the Wicked Witch of the West, we can return with some sort of proof to give to the Great Wizard so that he will grant our wishes." From far down the hall where I had pulled him, he added, his voice trailing, "However, lacking brains, I cannot absolutely, positively be certain of this or anything else."

After a long debate about the value of my suggestions that Scarecrow accurately intoned, they all went about preparing themselves for our next adventure.

WESTWARD HO

As the next morning dawned, Soldier led us back to Gate Guardian who unlocked our glasses and removed them.

As he led us out the front gate of the Emerald City, Dorothy asked Gate Guardian, "Which road leads to the Wicked Witch of the West?"

"There is no road," explained Gate Guardian. "We have no reason to go there so why bother building a road?"

"Because you have no reason to go there," Tin Woodman answered, quickly and sharply.

Gate Guardian moaned, "It was a rhetorical question."

Dumbfounded, each of us glanced at one another until Scarecrow offered this clarification. "By this, he means he did not expect an answer to the question for the answer was in the question itself."

"Oh ruff..." the rest of us responded harmoniously, now understanding.

"Then which way do we travel?" asked Lion.

"Why do you think they call her the Wicked Witch of the West?" Gate Guardian lamented. We were not sure if he was putting forth another rhetorical question that did not require a response so we gave him none. After a very long moment, he frowned at us and said, "Because she lives in the West! Get it?"

"Oh ruff..." we nodded our heads, realizing that that should have been our response.

Gate Guardian let out a very heavy sigh when he saw we were not going anywhere and pointed, "That way."

As we turned to face west, Dorothy asked, "How will we find the Wicked Witch?"

"Don't worry," Gate Guardian called after us as we skipped merrily away, "she'll find you, imprison you, and make you her slaves if she doesn't feast on you for dinner. Have a nice trip."

AS WE CONTINUED WEST we entered uncultivated hills where the ground was rough and there were no houses or farms to be seen anywhere.

"This is odd," said Tin Woodman, looking at the satin dress Dorothy still wore from the Emerald City. "It was green not long ago and now it has turned bright yellow."

"The ribbon around Toto's neck has also lost its green color and turned yellow," added Lion.

"It must be because we have left the Emerald City far behind where everything, including the people's skin, hair, and eyes are green as emeralds," said Scarecrow.

"Then we must be in the land of yellow," suggested Dorothy.

The hills were barren, so there were no trees to diffuse the glare of the bright setting sun in the west and soon Dorothy's, Lion's, and my own eyes grew tired of looking into it and we stopped to rest and fell asleep on the crunchy, dead grass.

MENACING OBSTRUCTIONS

We awoke the next morning to find Tin Woodman and Scarecrow standing where they stood awake all night. Although, oddly, a heap of forty hairy wolves with their heads cut clean off surrounded them.

"Hope you slept well," Tin Woodman said, leaning on the handle of his ax, the blade of which bathed in blood, formed a thick, gooey pool where it touched the ground.

"Where did these dead wolves come from?" Dorothy yawned and stretched.

"One would deduce from the evidence at hand," offered Scarecrow, "that the Wicked Witch of the West, which I overheard when we were in Emerald City, has only one eye but it is as powerful as a telescope. With this eye, she could see us coming from the direction of the Emerald City. Since no one has any good reason to come in this direction, she must have realized we intend to destroy her. Summoning her wolves, she sent them on a mission to attack us. However," he pointed to his head, "my conclusions are the product of a no-brainer, so I would not rely too heavily on anything I just said."

There was a very long moment of silence before Tin Woodman broke in with, "Good thing I sharpened my ax before we left. Their heads sliced off with one good swing each."

"More dead bodies," Dorothy sighed, getting to her feet. "I hope there is some sort of janitorial organization available to clean up this mess."

Leaving the dead wolves behind, we had not traveled far before the sky grew black with a flock of angry crows flapping thunderously toward us.

"Crows!" said Scarecrow. "My specialty. Everyone lay down next to me and I will scare them off."

"Is that it?" asked Lion. "You're going to just stand there as if you were on a pole in the field?"

"That's what scarecrows do, out in the wild and wooly cornfields in the country," answered Scarecrow with resounding determination.

As the crows approached, we all lay down at Scarecrow's feet. Scarecrow, for his part, stuck his arms out to the sides and froze in the position of a scarecrow on a pole in the middle of a cornfield. At first, it appeared to work for the crows held back for a moment.

"Fellow crows," said King Crow, hovering above us, "don't be afraid. He is not a real man, but clothes stuffed with straw and a painted face. The Wicked Witch of the West sent us here to pluck their eyes out and let's start with this one."

King Crow flew at Scarecrow, but surprisingly Scarecrow, jumping to one side, caught it by the throat, twisted its neck and it fell to the ground, dead. One by one the other thirty-nine crows came at Scarecrow and one by one, he broke their necks, killing them instantly, and soon we were under a blanket of dead crows.

Rising from the heap of crows, Dorothy lamented, "More dead things to clean up. I certainly would not want to be the custodian in the Land of Oz."

Tin Woodman turned to Scarecrow and said, "If you can so easily assassinate so many crows at once why didn't you attempt it when you were guarding the fields?"

"Ever try to strangle a crow with your arms tied to a pole? Now, if my employer had left me on the ground...," Scarecrow took a boxer's stance, moving his feet swiftly and gracefully back and forth while jabbing punches right and left with his burlap fists. "There would not be a crow in Oz that would come near my field."

Suddenly a terrible buzzing sound got our attention and we looked skyward at a huge swarm of bees.

"Tin Woodman," said Scarecrow, "you must pull the stuffing out of me and cover our companions with my straw so the bees will not find them."

Dorothy, Lion, and I lay down close together on the ground and Tin Woodman emptied Scarecrow, covering us with straw. When the bees arrived they found only Tin Woodman to attack. One after another, the bees drove their stingers at Tin Woodman. Clank, clank, clank, clank, clank. One after another, the bees broke their stingers against his solid tin body. Since bees cannot survive without their stingers, one by one, they fell dead in a heap at Tin Woodman's tin feet.

When the bee attack was over, Tin Woodman stuffed straw back into Scarecrow and he bounded to his feet.

"A good thing Dorothy stuffed you with extra straw," Tin Woodman said.

"It is also a good thing you are made of tin so you can fend off the bees," Scarecrow's painted face smiled as they shook each other's hand, triumphantly.

Dorothy, stepping daintily over and around the pile of dead bees and dead crows, bemoaned, "This land is your land."

"This land is our land," agreed the others.

"And it is a mess for you and not me," sighed Dorothy. "Dead things keep piling up everywhere. So untidy."

We again headed west but stopped when we saw dozens of spear-carrying men charging at us.

"These must be Winkies," Scarecrow affirmed, "for everyone knows the west is the land of the Winkies and the color of their clothing is yellow."

"I didn't know this," said Tin Woodman.

"Nor I," Dorothy shrugged.

"Ruff," I said, not having any knowledge of Winkies.

"Yellow Winkies," declared Lion. "How unappetizing."

"They don't look very friendly, either," said Dorothy, "and I think they mean to spear us with their sharp-tipped spears until we are dead as doornails."

Lion looked into their eyes. Even from a far distance, he saw fear in them. "They don't look very brave," he concluded matter-of-factly.

"Most likely slaves of the Wicked Witch of the West," said Scarecrow. "They must only be doing what she had ordered them to do, so, in a way, we can't blame them for killing us."

"Still," Dorothy stated a reasonable argument, "we don't have to die simply to appease them or the Wicked Witch of the West, do we?"

"Especially not at this point in our adventure," Scarecrow agreed. "It would be a very premature departure."

"Quick, everyone behind me," Lion commanded, and we quickly gathered behind him. When the Winkies drew near, Lion leaped at them and roared a tremendous roar. The Winkies were, as Lion had expected, not brave at all, and they immediately turned and squealed with fright as they ran back in the direction they came from.

"They will be getting a good whipping from the old Witch when they get back home, no doubt," said Scarecrow.

"At least we did not have to kill them," said Dorothy, relieved. "With so many of them, they would have made a bigger mess than the mess of the dead wolves, crows, and bees."

"However," Tin Woodman offered, "if the Winkies applied themselves as they were ordered to do, we would not have added much to the clutter, for I can be recycled into some other device, and Scarecrow's clothing could be used as rags and his straw used for bedding material. Only you, Lion, and Toto are made of flesh and blood. Since you and Toto are quite petite you would hardly be a chore to dispose of."

"That is somewhat comforting, for I do like a tidy world," replied Dorothy, "and leaving all these dead about is irritably disorderly." She brushed her satin dress and apron off and then slapped her hands clean of the pile of dead. "Shall we?" she said, skipping merrily westward.

Suddenly the sky ahead of us grew black again and we heard a thunderous sound of chirping and laughter in the distance. We stopped in our tracks and stared in awe and fear as huge, horrifying winged monkeys swooped down from the sky and attacked us.

Tin Woodman swung his ax, but the winged monkeys dodged and then flew behind him, grabbed him under his arms, and lifted him high into the air. They flew away with him and dropped him from high above down to the sharp rocks below, where he crashed with a loud thunk!

More winged monkeys flew at Scarecrow. He swung his soft, stuffed fists, but the winged monkeys were too quick and two of them took hold of each of his arms, pulling them off to the sides while others grabbed his straw, emptying his clothing until there was nothing left, and then they tossed the clothing up into the tall branches of a nearby tree.

Another swarm of winged monkeys swooped down around Lion and he roared and snapped his great teeth and slashed with his great paws, but the winged monkeys, flying overhead, dropped a heavy net over his body and then wrapped it so tight around him that he could no longer move a muscle. Once they had him secured, they carried him far, far into the west.

While all of this happened, I sprang up into Dorothy's arms to protect her. I barked fiercely at the winged monkeys circling us while Dorothy held me back tightly. One very large, very hairy, grinning Winged Monkey flew toward us, but as he reached us, he suddenly halted in midair, waving off the other winged monkeys.

"We cannot kill the girl or that lump of a creature she holds in her arms," the leader of the winged monkeys commanded. "She has been smacked on the forehead with a kiss from the fat lips of the Good Witch which gives her the Protection of Goodness and Niceness, a charm more powerful than the Wicked Witch's charm of Bad and Awful. However, we cannot break the Wicked Witch's powerful charm that binds us to execute her evil endeavors."

Dorothy, appearing more confused than frightened, asked, "So does this mean you can't kill us, or does it mean you're going to kill us anyway, even though you'll get fined or a slap on the wrist afterward?"

The leader of the winged monkeys floated to the ground and the rest of the winged monkeys settled down around us, looking confused. He appeared menacing, but at the same time, a little relieved for not having to kill us. At least not at this very moment. Still, I narrowed my eyes, gritted my teeth, and growled at each and everyone one of them, holding them at bay.

"Rather than haggling with this dilemma on our own," the leader of the winged monkeys suggested, "we'll seize them, but not harm them and take them to the Witch so she may sort out this unfortunate situation in her own manner."

"Good choice," said Dorothy. "For a moment I had doubts about your capability to make clear-cut decisions. This shows you do have good leadership qualities. I commend you."

"Ah, thank you," the leader of the winged monkeys frowned, puzzled.

The leader then ordered two smaller winged monkeys to clasp their hands together to form a sort of seat between them for Dorothy to sit on with me on her lap and off we flew higher than a kite to the castle of the Wicked Witch of the West.

CASTLE OF THE WICKED WITCH

When we arrived, the winged monkeys gently set Dorothy down in a standing position before the Wicked Witch of the West.

Oddly, we found the Witch, wearing a Golden Cap with rubies and diamonds encircling its brim, standing on her left foot with her right foot held high and muttering, "Zing-zang-whiz-it-clan-do-me-a-jig-jim-jam..." over and over with her eyes shut tight.

"Hey Witch," the leader of the winged monkeys shouted, tapping her on the shoulder. "We're back. You can stop that gibberish now."

The Wicked Witch of the West froze. With a patch over her bad eye, she opened her good eye and looked around. "What's this?" she asked, looking at Dorothy and I while slowly lowering her right foot.

"As you ordered," the leader of the winged monkeys said, "we have Lion tied up in a pen outside your window so you can use him as you please. Tin Woodman is all dented on top of sharp rocks and Scarecrow is scattered everywhere."

"This girl, she remains alive!" the Witch snarled and glared at us with her one good eye.

"We could not kill her as you commanded because the girl carries the Protection of Goodness and Niceness on her forehead," the leader of the winged monkeys explained. "So, as you see, we cannot harm a hair on her head or the hair of that scrawny, furry organism in her arms."

The Witch quickly raised her left foot high, shut her eye tight, and muttered frantically, "Bling-blam-what-cha-can-blam-bum..."

"Sorry, but that gibberish won't work anymore," the leader of the winged monkeys interrupted her. "You've already used the spell of the Golden Cap three times to get us to do bad and awful things for you. Three's the limit. You no longer have power over us. Bye-bye!"

Just like that off they flew, the chattering, flapping winged monkeys.

"Drats!" said the Witch, dropping her left foot down hard. She opened her good eye, placed her fists on her hips, and glared at us, her face tense and furious. I could feel Dorothy's body trembling as she held me. Then, looking at the spot on Dorothy's forehead, the Witch smacked her own forehead with the open palm of her hand. "What a revolting development this is," she grumbled.

I realized then that the Witch, as the leader of the winged monkeys said, was powerless to do anything to Dorothy as long as that spot on Dorothy's forehead remained. Although, as hard as I tried, whining and licking her face, I could not get Dorothy to understand this and she remained fearful of the old Witch.

The Witch stood back and looked us over, but when she saw the sparkly shoes on Dorothy's feet, she involuntarily gasped, "Crud! Those are some powerful..." She stopped suddenly and looked at Dorothy more keenly with her one good eye. Realizing Dorothy remained in fear of her, the Witch recomposed to her normal mean and spiteful demeanor.

"You will do as you're told," said the Witch, pushing my snout off to the side, and jutting her face inches from Dorothy's wide-eyed face. "Do you understand?" She raised an umbrella and threatened Dorothy with it.

"Certainly, ma'am," Dorothy's voice quivered. "Thanks for not killing me," she curtsied.

"You can thank me now, however..." She dropped the subject like a hot rock and then, stepping back again, she asked in a pleasant voice, "You wouldn't want to give those sparkly shoes to me, would you?"

"I never take them off," Dorothy answered in a meek, low voice.

"Feet get a little stinky?" The Witch winked her good eye; if you can interpret a single eye-opening and closing rapidly as winking.

"I don't know about that," Dorothy's voice quaked. Maybe Dorothy didn't, but I certainly did, remaining close in proximity to her feet much of the time. "However, my Aunt Em advised me to always wear shoes in case I step on a rusty nail."

"Phooey!" The old Witch grumbled, shaking her evil head. Then, muttering under her breath, she added, "I'm going to keep a close eye on those shoes. I'll get them yet. Yes-siree Bob!"

Dorothy was put to work cleaning the castle and making beds. When the Wicked Witch directed Dorothy into the kitchen, she warned, "Don't you dare splash any water near me when you wash dishes and scrub floors."

"Why?" Dorothy asked.

The Witch suddenly clasped her hands on the umbrella behind her back and rocked back and forth on her heels while gazing about the kitchen at nothing in particular. "No reason," she chirped innocently.

Dorothy went about the business of cleaning and scrubbing the castle in her typical carefree fashion, pleased to be alive.

When I felt the need to take myself for a walkie, I made my way out and down a winding stairway that led me into the yard behind the castle. There were no trees in sight, but after sniffing a bush, I raised my hind leg and set about placing my scent on it. Then, when the job was completed, I spied the Wicked Witch hefting a heavy harness, similar to ones worn by horses. I decided to follow her and see what she was up to, and she led me to this large gated corral, and inside the corral, I saw Lion.

"What do you intend to do with the harness?" Lion growled at her.

"This is so you can pull my chariot about the countryside while I pay unexpected visits to my enslaved Winkies," the Witch replied, coldly.

However, when the Witch got near the gate of the corral that held Lion, he roared in her face and she quickly jumped back with fear and astonishment.

"How dare you talk to me like that," she snapped angrily at him.

"You come near me with that harness and I will bite your head off," Lion roared again. "I am a Lion, not a horse."

"What's a horse?" the Witch asked with a bewildered look.

Lion appeared befuddled. "If you don't know what a horse is, why do you have a chariot?"

"What do you think enslaved Winkies are for besides a good meal?"

"Are they tasty?" Lion's eyes brightened and he smacked his great lips. "The Winkies, I mean."

"You'll never know because I will starve you unless you do as I command."

"I will do nothing of the kind. Now beat it!"

The Witch threw the harness to the ground in a furious rage and put her fists on her hips, eyeing him sternly. "In a day or two, you will have a change of heart, Lion." She then turned quickly and stomped away in bitter disappointment.

However, unknown to the Witch, Lion did not starve as expected. After I alerted Dorothy of Lion's whereabouts, she snuck food to him and fed him quite nicely when the Witch was out of sight.

Many days passed and Dorothy's spirit began to wane. "Oh, Toto," she confessed to me, "I do not think we will ever get back to Aunt Em or Kansas."

I did my best to cheer her up, chasing my tail for lack of anything else to chase or lapping her face with my tongue when she lay down to rest or sleep, but nothing I did alleviated her sorrow. It did not help either that the Wicked Witch followed her as she did her chores, threatening all the time to beat her with the umbrella if she did not do a good job. However, as often as the Witch raised the umbrella, not once did she strike her. I knew it was because of the spot on Dorothy's forehead, but Dorothy could never understand this and cowered with fear with each threat of a blow.

Then, one day when we were in the kitchen, I spied the Witch eyeing the sparkly shoes with a wicked gleam in her good eye.

Dorothy held in her hands two buckets, one filled with coal and the other with water as she lumbered her way to the stove. After Dorothy fed the coals to the belly of the stove, she lifted the heavy bucket of water to pour into the cauldron. In the process, a small amount of water spilled. As the water splattered to the floor, the Witch, in one quick motion, jumped back a step while, at the same time, popped the umbrella open, cowering behind it. Once Dorothy finished, the Witch stood and retracted the umbrella, smiling as though nothing had occurred. This was not the first time the Witch reacted in this manner while Dorothy handled water. It was then that I realized the Wicked Witch never went anywhere without the umbrella. I thought it odd for we had yet to see it rain in the Land of Oz since we arrived. However, Dorothy, her back usually turned to the Witch, remained oblivious to the Witch's response to spilled water and I had yet to understand its significance myself.

Before Dorothy ignited the coals to heat the water to wash dishes, the Witch stopped her. "More coal," the Witch said, narrowing her one good eye on Dorothy. "Bring another bucket. No, wait, make that two buckets filled to the brim with coal. Filled to the brim."

"I don't think we need that much coal. There's enough..." Dorothy argued but stopped when the Witch raised her umbrella. Fearful of the Witch striking her, Dorothy grabbed the two empty buckets and scurried out of the kitchen.

While Dorothy was gone, the Witch laid the umbrella down on the floor a short distance in front of the stove. She stood back from it, muttered gibberish, wiggled her fingers, and added snorting sounds, then, in a blink of an eye, the umbrella vanished.

I stared curiously at the spot where the umbrella had been, but when I started toward it to sniff it out, the Witch shoved me back with her smelly foot.

When Dorothy returned hefting the two buckets of coal, one in each hand, I noticed Dorothy's shoulders sag with the weight as she lumbered back to the stove.

"Dorothy, dear," the Witch twittered in a high-pitched, pleasant voice as Dorothy reached the location where the umbrella had been.

Just as Dorothy looked back over her shoulder, her foot slipped on something unseen and I knew immediately it was the invisible umbrella. Thrown off balance by the weight of the buckets of coal, she tumbled to the floor, landing hard on one knee and scattering coal everywhere. As she fell, one of her sparkly shoes flew off her foot, and the Witch raced toward it, grabbed it, and slipped it on her foot before Dorothy could gather herself and stand.

"Ah-hah!" the Witch cried in triumph, listing to the left, with one shoe giving more height than the other shoe.

"What is that supposed to mean?" Dorothy asked, wiggling the toes of her shoeless foot.

"It means," the Witch hesitated, "that I just need... a... the other one and I will have double the power of any witch around."

"Well, you won't get it," Dorothy spat back in anger, rubbing her bruised knee.

Infuriated with the Witch's behavior, I growled and snapped at her ankle, but she swung her sparkly shoe and hit me in the snout, knocking me backward. Dorothy now grew even angrier and bent to pick up some coals to throw at her. The Witch quickly reversed her gibberish, wiggled her fingers, and snorted, unveiling the umbrella. She reached for the umbrella and sprang it wide open in time to deflect the hurled coals. When Dorothy's hands emptied, the Witch retracted the umbrella and raised it as though to strike her before Dorothy bent to pick up more coals. Raising her arms to shield the blow, Dorothy backed into the stove and jostled the cauldron of water. The caldron rocked, sloshing water over its edge and onto the floor at Dorothy's feet. The Witch reacted instinctively to the splashing water by hopping back and popping the umbrella wide open and ducking behind its circular shield. It was then I realized why the Witch went nowhere without her umbrella. For some strange reason, she was terrified of liquid. Anxious to test my theory, I quickly sprang into action. With a burst of speed, I raced up to her, lifted my hind leg, and sent a stream of warm bodily fluid over her ankle.

"Oh no!" the Witch wailed. "My foot it's... it's dissolving." My bodily fluid caused some chemical reaction that dissolved her foot from the ankle down into a small pile of brown dust and the Witch now hobbled on one foot with the sparkly shoe. "How could you let this furball spray me, knowing I will dissolve when wet?"

Dorothy demanded, "How in tarnation would I know you will dissolve when wet when wetness is universally appealing to most?"

"Your puny comrade has more brains than you," the Witch retorted, hopping in a circle. I had to agree with her there.

While I had the chance, I took the tip of the umbrella that hung down near me, clamped my teeth onto it, and yanked it from the Witch's grip. I then ran with it over to Dorothy, dropped the umbrella at her feet, and barked, "The Witch is now defenseless. Quickly, grab a bucket, fill it with water, and toss it on the Witch. This will dissolve her to nothing."

Even though my assumption was correct, Dorothy hushed me, saying, "Quiet, Toto, I'm thinking." Dorothy was never one to make rash decisions, but eventually, she did accept my suggestion. In rapid succession, she picked up an empty bucket, dipped it into the cauldron of water, turned to face the Witch, and stood poised to douse her.

"Don't you dare toss that water on me!" The Witch hopped backward. "I'll dissolve into nothingness."

"Then there won't be much of a mess to clean up, will there?" Dorothy said, stepping toward the Witch. "Leaving dead bodies about is so untidy and this especially goes for a dead body in the kitchen. How unsanitary that would be!" With that, Dorothy launched the water over the Witch and, sure enough, she began to dissolve.

"I'm dissolving," the Witch moaned, becoming more and more diminutive. "I'm dissolving... I'm... I'm... dissolved!"

Soon there was nothing left of the Witch, but a neat pile of brown dust beneath her clothing. Even as diminutive as I am, I could now stand over her and look down at her remains.

"Another one bites the dust," said Dorothy, slapping her hands clean. "Oh my."

RESCUE, RESTORE, REUNITE

Now that the Witch was no longer a witch or anything resembling a living creature, Dorothy separated the sparkly shoe from the pile of dust, shook it clean, and replaced it on her foot. Removing the Witch's clothing and dropping them into a dustbin, she then took up a broom and a dustpan and swept the Witch up, whistling while she worked.

Once she had cleaned the kitchen of the Witch, we ventured down the spiral stairway and out into the courtyard. First, Dorothy unlocked the gate to the corral and freed Lion, and then she summoned all the Yellow Winkies together and announced she had killed the Wicked Witch. Even though she failed to state my involvement, quick thinking, and resourcefulness, I am not one to bicker over details and let her negligence slide.

"My-gosh, you're good," many cried of Dorothy's ability to do away with Wicked Witches and other annoying creatures in her path. "Enslave us, enslave us," many moaned, holding their hands to their hearts in awe and appreciation.

"Sorry, but I'm just a little girl," sighed Dorothy. "I don't enslave anyone or anything."

"So what's the deal with your minion?" asked one, referring to me.

"Oh? Well...?" replied Dorothy, confused by the exact aspect of our relationship.

"No more enslaving," shouted another of the Winkies. "We're through with being enslaved. We are all free to do as we please as soon as we can find someone to lead us and tell us specifically what it is we're supposed to be doing."

"Dorothy, Dorothy…" the chant began. "Lead us, lead us!"

"I suppose being your leader is not exactly enslaving you and I think I could be your leader for a little while," said Dorothy, modestly, thinking something through. "If you will follow me, I can lead you to where my friends are so we may bring them back and repair them."

The Winkies thought that was a good start and we set off immediately to find our friends with some of the largest of the male Winkies to help carry them back if they were incapable of walking. However, size is relative in the Land of Oz. The largest of the Winkies who accompanied us were no larger than Dorothy, but none as petite.

We traveled for two days before we came to the rocky area where Tin Woodman lay broken and in disrepair. His joints were rusted and his tin body cracked and torn open in several places. Dorothy asked the Winkies if they knew of a good tinsmith and one, named Tim Smith, said that he was a very capable tinsmith and he had some very capable coworkers to boot. That's if Tin Woodman needed tin boots. Pleased that Tim Smith offered to repair Tin Woodman, she asked the larger of the Winkies to hoist Tin Woodman off the sharp rocks and carry him back to the castle. Over the next three days, Tim Smith and his tinsmiths hammered, ground, soldered, filed, and oiled until Tin Woodman was back in good shape. Although not as polished as he would have liked, since there were many tin patches over his body, he did not complain since he lacked the heart to do so.

Tin Woodman thanked Tim Smith, his tinsmiths, the Winkies, and Dorothy for saving his life. "It feels so good to be rescued, refurbished, and reassembled." Tin Woodman gaily pounded his tin body with his tin fists producing a hollow rumble within. He was even more pleased when Tim Smith presented him with his sharpened ax.

"My wife, Golda Smith," said Tim Smith, "is a goldsmith and she has fastened a handle made of pure gold for your ax."

When Tin Woodman took the ax in his hands, he nearly toppled over, not expecting it to be as heavy as it was with a handle of pure gold. "I will just have to get used to it," he told Tim and Golda Smith, not having the heart to tell them the pure gold handle makes the ax's balance disproportional, and that he would prefer to have more weight on the end he swings away from his body.

While everyone stood about thanking each other, I barked with some urgency.

I just don't know what is wrong with humans. Dorothy, Lion, and Tin Woodman just stood there staring down at me dumbly even though I was reminding them that Scarecrow was still out there scattered about somewhere and we needed to find him and bring him back. "R-r-r ruff-ruff-ruff-ruff!" I repeated my appeal until Tin Woodman finally sided with me.

"We are not complete without our friend Scarecrow," said Tin Woodman.

When it was clear to me that they were not about to budge an inch, I barked, "Come on guys, we need to find Scarecrow or what is left of him."

Still, it seemed like forever before Dorothy responded to my urgent plea. "I know," she said, "let's find Scarecrow, and bring him back for repairs." Boy, sometimes you have to hit humans over the head before they listen to you.

We returned to the scene of the crime and found the tall tree where the winged monkeys had scattered Scarecrow's clothing. The clothes were very high up in the tree branches and the tree was much too slippery for anyone to climb. No one knew what to do. Of course, it fell to me to come up with a solution.

"Ruff-ruff-ruff-ruff!" I said and then gnawed at the bark of the tree to demonstrate.

Tin Woodman stared at me with a look of annoyance at first, but then finally, after a long moment, agreed with my suggestion. "I know what to do," he said to the others. "I will chop the tree down with my ax so we can recover Scarecrow's clothing after it falls to the ground."

That's what I just said, but did I get credit for coming up with the idea first? No. Everyone crowded around Tin Woodman, practically stepping on me, congratulating and patting him on the back.

With the first swing of the unbalanced ax, Tin Woodman missed the tree entirely and brought the ax around in a full circle, nearly slicing those near him in half. Fortunately, for me, he missed me by about four feet above my head.

"I'll get the hang of it yet," Tin Woodman said, not having the heart to blame the unbalanced ax for the near misfortune.

Finally, with a few steady swings, the tree fell and Dorothy and the Winkies recovered Scarecrow's clothing and carried these back to the castle where the Winkies stuffed them with fresh, clean straw.

"Thanks," Scarecrow said, bounding to his feet, though a bit unsteady. "Even if I had a brain I doubt I could have managed to think about how to recover, reconstruct, re-stitch, and re-stuff myself without your help." Scarecrow stepped around and over me shaking each hand all the while overlooking me in his appreciation. Whatever.

It was pleasant enough making the castle our temporary home now that we were all reunited, but it was not long before Dorothy grew sad again. While she sat on her bed with me on her lap, rubbing my back, she gave me a forlorn look and said, "I do miss Aunt Em and Uncle Henry. We really must try to get back to Kansas."

Even though I was happy where I was, being the top dog since there were no other dogs in the Land of Oz, I did not want Dorothy to be sad. After considering it for a moment, I barked, "Okay, fine. Then we must return to the Emerald City and explain to the Wizard that we did as he asked and now it was his turn to comply with our wishes."

Dorothy looked off into the distance and replied in her usual, sweet fashion, "Hush, Toto, I'm trying to think."

What did she have to think over? Still, I gave her time and remained quiet as she thought it through.

"I know, Toto," she said in a burst of excitement, jumping to her feet and spilling me to the floor, "we must return to the Emerald City and demand that the Wizard grant our wishes. After all, we did kill the Witch for him. Come, Toto, we must tell the others." She nearly trampled me as she fled through the door.

When Tin Woodman, Scarecrow, and Lion heard we were going back to the Great Wizard to claim our reward for snuffing out the Wicked Witch of the West, they grew very excited and each moaned with delight.

"A heart."

"A brain."

"The courage."

Dorothy led us to the kitchen where she filled her wicker basket with food.

Looking around, I noticed the Golden Cap that the Witch had worn the day we arrived. It was on a bench in the corner and I went over and sniffed at it. Since the Witch had worn it while casting a spell, I had a suspicion that it might be of some use or significance, so I picked it up in my mouth and carried it to Dorothy.

"How pretty," said Dorothy, patting me on the head in gratitude. "It has very nice diamonds and rubies around its brim." She put the Golden Cap on her head, adjusting it. "Not too tight, not too loose, it fits just right."

When the Winkies heard we were leaving they came and begged Tin Woodman to stay and rule them. "I have to accompany Dorothy in case she'll need me to chop a path through the forest," he answered, not having the heart to tell them the real reason he wanted to go and see the Wizard of Oz.

Then they turned to Lion and asked him to stay and rule them. "I may be needed to protect Dorothy in the event bad creatures abound in her path," he answered, lacking the courage to tell them the real reason he wanted to go and see the Wizard of Oz.

Then they asked Scarecrow, and all he did was raise his hands in the air, looking confused, not having the brains to think of an excuse for not staying and becoming their ruler.

I suppose the Winkies knew it would be hopeless to ask me to stay and rule them since the others had already declined. However, I wished they had, for I would have considered the offer. It would be wonderful ruling over the Winkies and watching them scurry about every time I barked orders. Then again, what would Dorothy do without me? It was my responsibility to guard her, steer her in the right direction, remain a loyal life companion, and make her laugh. If Dorothy wanted to return to Kansas, it was my obligation to accompany her. I would follow her to the ends of the Earth, or anywhere if it would get us out of Kansas again.

I quickly felt squeezed in by the crowd as the Winkies gathered around us and presented us with gifts. Both Lion and I received collars made of gold and Dorothy got a diamond-studded bracelet. Then they presented Tin Woodman with a silver oilcan inlaid with precious jewels and gave Scarecrow a gold-headed cane to steady his walk. Made of straw, he tended to flop from side to side with the slightest breeze.

We each felt obligated to give a little speech. Dorothy spoke first, then Tin Woodman, followed by Lion. I chose to go last, but when Scarecrow began, his speech went on and on with no particular end in sight. For someone with no brain, he had a lot to get off of his mind, if he had one, that is. After Scarecrow's laborious speech, it became my turn. However, I could see in the Winkies' weary faces that they had enough speeches for one afternoon, so I decided to skip mine for their sake.

WHICH WAY IS WHICH

Since we traveled west to get to the castle of the now-expired Wicked Witch, the Winkies suggested we head toward the sun that was rising in the east. However, the land was flat and completely barren of any noticeable landmarks so that, when the sun rose overhead at noon, we lost any reference to guide us.

"We will just have to stop and rest until the sun moves further across the sky," said Scarecrow. "Everyone but me knows the sun settles in the west. So, in the afternoon, if we keep the sun to our backs it should guide us to the east where the Emerald City lays. Or is it lies?"

"If you don't know that the sun settles in the west," Dorothy asked, "how did you come up with the plan to travel with the sun to our backs?"

Scarecrow threw his hands up in despair. "Beats me."

"Is that a request?" asked Tin Woodman and Lion, making fists and waving them near Scarecrow.

"I think not," said Dorothy. "I believe it is merely a figure of speech." Tin Woodman and Lion unclenched their fists, looking rather disappointed. "Still, I think we should follow Scarecrow's advice once the sun continues its westward direction."

As we waited, dark clouds swiftly moved in overhead, obscuring the sun from view.

"Oh, drats!" said Dorothy. "Now how are we going to find our way without the sun on our backs?"

"We could go this way ruff-ruff," Scarecrow, Lion, Tin Woodman, and I said, each of us pointing in opposite directions, confounding

Dorothy. For her part, she decided to follow the wind. She spat into the air to see which direction it would go. Unfortunately, the spit reversed its course and hit her smack in the eye.

"Ah corn-husk," Dorothy cursed, wiping her eye. She then made a guess. "Let's try this way."

For the next couple of days, with the sun hidden behind thick clouds, we wandered in one way and then another until we all grew tired and flopped on the grass, hopelessly lost.

"We're lost," cried Scarecrow. "Without a brain, I am useless to help us find our way."

"If I had a heart it would be broken right about now," bemoaned Tin Woodman.

"I lack the courage to go on aimlessly," lamented Lion, "and would rather just sit here and die."

I too was tired and lacked the energy to even snap my teeth or throw a paw at a butterfly circling my head. I just lay in a heap with my tongue hanging out, panting.

Dorothy sat Indian style plucking at the petals of a daisy while moaning repeatedly, "There's no place like... whatever."

Suddenly I caught sight of something small scurrying through the grass not far away. A mouse, I thought to myself. That's it! Mice! Remembering what the Queen Mouse had said, I leaped up onto Dorothy's lap and licked her mouth.

"Ca-phooey!" said Dorothy, pushing me away and wiping her mouth. "That's worse than spit in your eye. Besides, your breath smells."

Undaunted, I turned and hopped back into the grass and sniffed around until I got the scent of the mouse. Finding it not far away, I dashed like lightning and snatched up the mouse between my teeth. "Squeak, squeak, squeak..." it cried out as I trotted back to Dorothy and deposited it into her lap. I sat back and nodded toward the mouse, which was too frightened to move an inch. Dorothy frowned at the mouse and then at me. I barked, "Don't you remember what the Queen of Mice said? If you whistle they will return to help us." All I got for this was an admonishment from Dorothy.

"Hush, Toto. You're scaring the poor little creature," she said, gentling stroking the mouse shivering with fear in her lap.

I flopped on the ground and covered my nose with my paws, annoyed by Dorothy's lack of understanding. If I had lips that could purse, I would take a stab at whistling for the Queen of Mice myself.

"Squeak!" the mouse squeaked fearfully.

"Tweet!" replied Dorothy unconsciously in return.

"Ruff," I said, encouraging Dorothy, now that she was on the right track.

"Tweet," Dorothy repeated with a look of surprise.

She looked at the mouse, then at me, and back at the mouse. She then leaped to her feet excitedly, letting the mouse sail from her lap and down onto the ground. The mouse, a bit dazed from the unexpected events and awkward landing, staggered a bit before disappearing back into the grass as fast as its little feet could carry it. I looked after it for a moment before a shrill, piercing sound from above startled me and I backed away hurriedly and looked up at Dorothy. She had two fingers on either side of her mouth and, as she blew hard, she again produced that same shrill, piercing sound that you could hear for miles around.

"Who are you trying to annoy?" asked Scarecrow, covering his painted ears with his burlap-gloved hands.

"I'm whistling," explained Dorothy, "so I can get the Queen of Mice to help us find our way."

"With that sound, you will most likely wake the dead witches."

Dorothy disregarded Scarecrow's comment and blew again.

"There's a ringing in my ears," said Tin Woodman, covering them.

Lion was on the ground next to me as we both covered our ears with our paws.

"I'm here," squeaked the Queen of Mice from a distance. "You can cut that god-awful noise."

"Oh, Queen of Mice," said Dorothy, her face flushed from the exertion of whistling. "I'm happy you responded so quickly."

"Better I do than go deaf," she replied as she scurried up to us. "What do you want? I mean, how may I help you?" She mustered a smile, after shaking off the ringing in her ears.

"We're trying to find our way back to the Emerald City, but we don't have the sun to guide us east," explained Dorothy.

"Use your noggin," the Queen replied, jutting her nose toward the top of Dorothy's head. Dorothy's eyes turned upward, but she shook her head, not understanding. "The Golden Cap. It's got a charm attached to it."

Dorothy felt with her hand around the cap, but then shrugged, confused.

"It's not physically attached, but there is a charm you can read inside of it that will bring the winged monkeys."

"Not the winged monkeys ruff-ruff-ruff!" all of us gasped and huddled together for dear life.

"Tut-tut," said the Queen. "You need not be afraid of the winged monkeys if you have command of the Golden Cap. They must obey the charm of the Golden Cap three times and, as I can see, having them fly you to the Emerald City will save a lot of time. You do realize you are going in the opposite direction."

"I'll give it a try," said Dorothy. She took the Golden Cap off her head and read the inscription on a tag at the back. "Wash in cold water with items of similar color and jewels. Hang to dry."

"That's the laundry instructions," said the Queen, rolling her eyes. "Look around the inside edge."

"Right," said Dorothy, looking again.

"Well, we got to be on our way," said the Queen.

After thanking her and saying goodbye to all the mice, Dorothy memorized the charm and placed the Golden Cap back onto her head. She raised her left foot and muttered, "Zing-zang, jittery bang-bang, olf, olf, olf." Then lowering that foot, she raised her right foot and muttered, "Oh blah dee, oh blah dah, life goes on, ka-ping, dingle-ling." Now with both feet on the ground, she finished with, "Here we go, loop dee loop, ka-pow, wow, wow."

"Catchy tune," remarked Lion. "Sort of."

Just then, we heard the tremendous flapping of wings as the winged monkeys swooped toward us.

"That charm sounds different every time I hear it," said the leader of the winged monkeys. "How can we be of service?"

"Can you fly us to the Emerald City?"

"One way or round trip?"

"One way, I hope," said Dorothy.

Before we knew it, the winged monkeys had lifted us all into the air and we sailed out of the barren lands and over beautiful fields and forests. Looking down, I just could not imagine why we would want to leave this place, except for the dark forest, horrible creatures, and wicked witches that seem to have it in for us for no good reason. Still, for better or worse, there was nothing like it in Kansas.

RETURN TO EMERALD CITY

"Here you are," said the leader of the winged monkeys, letting us down gently in front of the gate of Emerald City. "Just garble some more of the charm if you need us again." With that, he led the winged monkeys away.

Dorothy turned and, this time, she remembered to push the button to alert the Gate Guardian so he may open the gate.

Gate Guardian opened the gate with a look of astonishment upon seeing us. "Goodness gracious great balls of fire," he shouted and fell back on the seat of his pants. After Scarecrow and Tin Woodman helped him back to his feet, he added, breathlessly, "You're back."

"Of course, we're back," frowned Dorothy, her hands on her slender hips. "What did you expect?"

"The Wicked Witch of the West never lets anyone leave," Gate Guardian gulped. "And there are many perils along the way that hamper one's existence."

Tin Woodman stepped forward and said with an air of aloofness, "What's a Wicked Witch, winged monkeys, stinging bees, crows, wolves, and Winkies with sharp spears to us?" Breathing on his tin fist, he polished it smugly over his chest.

"The Wicked Witch of the West, what became of her?" asked Gate Guardian.

"Doused her with a bucket of water," said Scarecrow, his arm resting arrogantly on Tin Woodman's shoulder.

"All that is left of her is a pile of dust," Lion gloated, looking off in the distance as though what we had experienced was a trifle inconsequential.

I barked coolly, "Just a warm stream of bodily fluid and a dash of water from a bucket is all that was needed. Any dog would have concluded this easily enough." I looked up into the sky at nothing in particular attempting to appear nonchalant like the others, but the Gate Guardian took no notice of me as he was too busy gaping at my companions.

"And the rest?" he asked, eyes wide and mouth gaping. "The others you mention?"

Dorothy casually brushed back her hair with the tips of her fingers. "The Winkies we spared and are safe and free at last," she spoke airily. "However, there is some tidying up to do, with all the dead we left in our wake."

I barked, "Don't you think it's about time you let us in?"

Like a fool, Gate Guardian stared down at me for a very long moment before turning to the box of glasses. "We must tell the Great Wizard immediately," he said, taking out glasses and passing them to each of us. "Quickly, put these on so I can lock them and let you in. Hurry. Hurry."

Of course, I needed assistance from Dorothy and I stood still as she placed mine over my eyes with the chain going around the back of my head.

As we strode with pride through the Emerald City, Gate Guardian repeated our accomplishments to all those we passed and soon it seemed that the entire population of the city was walking behind us in wonderment and awe.

Soldier met us at the door of the Palace and rushed inside. However, instead of taking us straight to see the Great Wizard, he led us to Girl who again guided us to our rooms.

"Hasn't the Great Wizard been told of our accomplishments?" Dorothy asked Girl.

Girl curtsied and replied, "Soldier went at once to inform the Great Wizard."

"And...?"

"He has not given a response."

"None?"

"Nothing. Nada. Zilch," Girl curtsied again.

"Well, what a fine how-do-you-do this is," puzzled Dorothy. "After all we've done and been through."

Scrutinizing Wizard's refusal to acknowledge our deeds, I barked, "Is the Great Wizard jealous because we have achieved a feat even the Magnificent and Malicious Wizard himself is incapable of accomplishing?"

Girl, who had turned and was on her way out the door, did not respond, apparently not having heard me.

Dorothy looked down at me, shrugged, and then flopped back onto the bed and went fast to sleep, snoring loudly. With nothing better to do, I cuddled up next to her and snoozed away.

WE SPENT THE NEXT FEW days in our rooms without a single word from the Great Wizard. Dorothy, having waited long enough, called for the others to gather in her room so she would not have to bristle with displeasure alone.

"What are we to do?" Scarecrow moaned.

"We can't stand around here forever," complained Tin Woodman, who like Scarecrow, had stood forever in his room until Dorothy called for him.

Dorothy stood glaring out the door, her arms folded tightly across her chest. She scrunched up her face in frustration while tapping her foot.

"You would think he could have at least sent a thank you note for killing the Wicked Witch of the West," said Lion, frowning his disappointment.

Dorothy had no answer. Instead, she tapped, scrunched up her face, and tapped some more, fuming.

The others let out a heavy sigh of frustration and then sat or stood silently brooding.

Tap-tap, crunch, tap-tap, fume!

Having had enough of all this waiting, I turned to the Golden Cap on a table by the bed. Realizing we could employ the Golden Cap in some manner, I snatched it up and took it to Dorothy. I sat on my haunches in front of her with my paws in the air and the Golden Cap in my mouth. She did not notice me at first until I dropped it at her feet and barked, "We can threaten the Wizard that, if he does not call for us soon, we will use the Golden Cap to summon the winged monkeys and have them rough him up."

Dorothy, looking down at me, picked up the Golden Cap and rephrased my suggestion to the others. "I know what I'll do. I will send word to the Wizard that, if he does not call for us soon, I'll use the charm of the Golden Cap to beckon the winged monkeys to manhandle him. Or monkey-handle him."

Dorothy called Girl and asked that she relate her threat to the Great Wizard, and it was not long before Girl returned with Soldier, their faces flushed and appearing alarmed.

"Oh, please don't call the winged monkeys," pleaded Girl.

"The Wizard's prior experience with them was not a pleasant one," added Soldier, his voice trembling.

"Well...?" demanded Dorothy, fuming, tapping, and crunching.

"First thing in the morning," said Soldier.

"At nine o'clock, he requests your presence," said Girl.

Then they backed out the door, curtsying, and bowing, too afraid to make eye contact with any of us.

"Wait until tomorrow?" asked Dorothy, with growing suspicion. "I wonder what he has up his sleeve," she added, pulling up her sleeves, her dainty fists tightly wound and her face crunched while her foot tapped.

"I wonder ruff-ruff?" each of us remarked as one, wondering. We all sighed, waited, and wondered and waited some more.

UNMASKING DECEPTION

At exactly nine o'clock the next morning, Soldier returned and commanded, "It's time for all of you to go to the Throne Room."

"I've already been," replied Dorothy with a satisfactory sigh. "Thank you, though, for asking."

"Toto and I have already taken ourselves for a walkie," Lion spoke up for the two of us.

"We never go," declared Tin Woodman and Scarecrow simultaneously. "No need to."

"No, no, not *that* throne room," said Soldier. "The Throne Room of the Magnificent, Malicious, Great and Wonderful Oz."

"Oh, that Throne Room ruff-ruff-ruff," we all responded, understanding.

We all had given up trying to imagine what to expect and decided to let things fall where they may. After all the challenges we had faced, we were confident we would achieve what we came for, one way or another, even if the Great Wizard was not about to live up to his promises. With that carefree attitude, we hummed merrily to a tune oddly embedded in our collective memories as we skipped, trotted, sauntered, and clanked behind Soldier to the Throne Room.

However, when we stood before the door of the Throne Room, doubt and trepidation suddenly seized everyone.

"What terrible form will the Great Wizard assume when he greets us this time?" asked Tin Woodman, rattling metallically from head to foot. "Not a horrible rhinoceros, I beg."

"I hope it is a beautiful woman," said Scarecrow, mindlessly pulling and dropping straw from his chest onto the floor. "I would not like anything to do with fire."

"Pull yourself together," growled Lion. "You'll empty yourself before we go in."

"Oh, yes," said Scarecrow, gathering the straw at his feet and re-stuffing himself. "But, if I recall, it was a flame that nearly burned your tail off."

Lion gulped, recalling his time in the Throne Room. "Like you, I would be a little susceptible to fire if ignited at a delicate location."

Dorothy said, "The big head that greeted me was not so frightening, but just a tad rude."

"Then, after you, Dorothy," said Tin Woodman, ducking behind her.

"Ah..." said Dorothy, having doubts as she stared at the Throne Room door before her. "Maybe Scarecrow should lead us." She reached back and jerked him forward, taking a position directly behind him.

"I think it will be best if Lion leads us," whispered Scarecrow nervously.

Before Lion knew it, Scarecrow, Dorothy, and Tin Woodman were in a line behind him, pushing him forward. Each time someone found himself or herself in the lead, that one would quickly dodge and move to the back of the line. This went on for a good five minutes and I got a little dizzy watching them.

I barked, "Stop being so foolish and stand behind me." I took the lead but, as I trotted toward the Throne Room door, they continued to shuffle and scramble, not wanting to be the first in line behind me as we entered.

As I led them into the Throne Room, we found it practically empty. No large, terrifying anything to be seen anywhere. Just curved walls, a domed ceiling, a circular floor, and an empty throne. We gazed around suspiciously, but before we could draw any conclusion, a voice seemingly coming from the domed ceiling spoke to us in a somber tone.

"Why have you come?"

"Who's up there?" Tin Woodman questioned in a quivering voice.

"Who do you think?" the voice grumbled back.

Tin Woodman offered a guess, "Wizard?"

The voice roared, "It is I, the one and only Magnificent, Terrifying Wizard of Oz!"

"What happened to Malicious?" asked Scarecrow, afraid of the answer.

"I thought terrifying sounded a bit more temperate than malicious," the voice boomed. "I like fear to be part of my essence, but I don't necessarily want to harm anyone."

"Very kind of him," Tin Woodman mumbled to the others, pointing a tin finger skyward. "The Wizard, I mean." We all nodded in agreement.

"What do you want from me?" We looked down when the voice now appeared to come from the empty throne. We tried to look behind it to see if anyone was back there, but were startled when the voice snapped angrily, "Well...?"

Dorothy, having experienced his rudeness before, became suddenly defiant. "We killed the old witch and we want you to deliver on your promises," she demanded, stomping her foot daintily.

"We disposed of her," said Tin Woodman, following Dorothy's defiant lead.

"Dissolved her," chimed Scarecrow, confidently.

"Laid her to waste," roared Lion.

"Ruff!" I barked, providing my description of what happened to the Wicked Witch.

"Well...!" replied the voice, softer, meeker, and a little taken back. "All on your own?"

"No more questions," Dorothy narrowed her eyes on the empty throne. "We want results."

"I want brains," Scarecrow insisted. "Lots of them!"

"I, a heart," Tin Woodman commanded. "A big, soft heart!"

"For me, courage," Lion specified with a roar. "Courage beyond compare!"

"I want to go home!" Dorothy stomped her foot again. "Home to Kansas."

"Ruff!" I sided with Dorothy.

"Where's you're proof?" the voice asked. Show me proof!"

"Here," said Dorothy, removing the Golden Cap from her head and holding it out toward the throne. "The Wicked Witch of the West used its powers to command the winged monkeys to attack us. She would not give it up willingly, would she?"

"How do I know you didn't buy it off the rack?" questioned the voice. "It could be an imitation made in China."

"This is genuine," Dorothy retorted. "We used it to have the winged monkeys fly us back from the castle and we'll use it to summon the winged monkeys to dispatch you if you don't ante up with results."

"Let me have it so I can see if it's the Real McCoy," suggested the voice. "Then we'll negotiate."

"No negotiations," Dorothy stomped her foot. "We demand what you promised!"

The argument with the voice going nowhere, I lost interest and decided to sniff about. Suddenly I got a whiff of a human. A human that did not smell like Dorothy, but more like Uncle Henry. An old, musty sort of human smell. As the others continued with their demands, I put my nose to the ground and followed the scent. The scent led me to a large screen in the shadows off to the side of the circular room. As I drew near, I thought I could hear a voice behind it, a voice not unlike the voice coming from the throne, but much weaker. When I reached the screen, I sat back and studied it, my ears perked and my cold nose sniffing. There seemed to be someone hiding behind the screen intoning the same words simultaneously as the words we heard booming into the room. Curious as to who might be back there, I clamped my teeth on a corner of the screen and pulled back. As I did this, the screen fell, revealing a nervous, little bald man at the controls of a large board with flashing lights and speaking into an amplifying horn of some sort. At first, the little man did not notice me so I clamped my teeth onto his pant leg and pulled. He turned around, surprised and terrified.

"Go! Shoo! Beat it!" The little man tried to shake me loose, but I would not budge. "Please, go away," he pleaded, shaking his leg and me with it. Finally, I let loose and barked and barked until the others turned and gaped at the little man. One by one, they drew closer, eyeing him curiously.

The little man continued to speak into the amplifying horn, unaware of the others approaching him.

"Wizard?" asked Tin Woodman, towering over him, his ax gripped in his hands.

The little man looked behind him at Tin Woodman and the others, then quickly spoke into the horn, his voice booming through the room. "I am the Magnificent and Malicious...."

Dorothy cut him off. "No, you're not. Magnificent, I mean. You're just a little old man pretending to be something you're not."

"I expected," said Scarecrow, "someone with a little more stature."

"And with more gumption," added Lion.

"A phony!" Tin Woodman clanked his ax handle on his open tin hand menacingly.

"I could swallow you whole," Lion bared his massive teeth and snapped.

"Ger-r-r-r-r," I growled, growling.

"Humph!" said Dorothy, indignantly, her arms folded tightly over her chest and blowing up from a corner of her mouth at hair dangling loosely from her forehead. "We've been had."

The little man pleaded, "Please don't let it be known who or what I am. I've got a good gig going here and I don't want to lose it."

Dorothy snarled. "You're nothing but a pretense of a wizard and Pretense-Wizard is what we'll call you from now on." She had a bit of mean spirit in her that surfaced now and again when she did not get her way. "Trickery, is it?" She eyed him sternly.

"That is true," Pretense-Wizard had to admit. "But you and everyone in the Land of Oz were gullible enough. Up until now, at least."

We all looked at one another, nodding our heads as we each, in turn, voiced our sentiments.

"He baited us."

"And we took it."

"Then swallowed it whole."

"Hook, line, and sinker."

"Ruff."

The little man shook nervously. "Fine. I'll do whatever you ask. Let's just keep the truth about me between us, okay?"

Scarecrow gave out a huge sigh, flopped on the floor, and rested his chin on his gloved hands. "If you are not a true wizard then you cannot grant us our wishes."

Pretense-Wizard put a finger to his chin in thought. "Tell me again, your wishes."

"Why?" fumed Scarecrow.

Pretense-Wizard waved his hand at the controls behind him. "I like to tinker. Tinkering allowed me to become whatever I wanted others to see me as and by tinkering I may be able to come up with something for each of you."

"Then, in a way, you are a wizard," concluded Tin Woodman. "A mechanical wizard."

"If so," said Scarecrow, "I wish to have brains. Lots of brains."

"Me, too," said Lion. "Big, juicy, tasty brains." He wet his lips and smacked them.

"Not to eat," said Scarecrow, aghast. "Brains to think, to dream, formulate, invent..."

"Sorry," said Lion, rubbing his large stomach with his paw. "I suppose I'm a bit famished at the moment and the thought of food is the only thing that came to mind."

"...conceive, rationalize, scrutinize, hypothesize, theorize, conjure..," continued Scarecrow.

Pretense-Wizard asked Lion, "What was your wish?"

"I wish for courage!" Lion roared fiercely. "So I will fear no one or nothing."

Sarecrow went on, "... imagine, regard, envision, perceive, evaluate..."

"Enough already ruff-ruff!" we all shouted, unable to think with Scarecrow's continued rambling.

Scarecrow stopped, his finger in the air, and responded, softly, hesitantly, "Brains to know when to be quiet?"

"I'll see what I can do in the brain department," sighed Pretense-Wizard. Scarecrow's painted face smiled with delight. "However, brains alone do not make you smart or clever. It is what you experience, and what you learn from it."

"I'd still like to have some brains," said Scarecrow. "It's awfully empty up here." He tapped his gloved finger against his burlap head and it made no sound.

"Possibly tomorrow I will have brains for you."

Turning to Lion, Pretense-Wizard said, "You may already possess courage. Admitting you're afraid takes courage. I do not know of any person or animal that is not afraid at some point in time. Even though you are afraid, that does not mean you lack the courage to face your fears."

"Still," said Lion. "I would feel much better if you'll supply me with courage I can take back with me. As a backup, if nothing more."

Pretense-Wizard nodded. "Tomorrow."

Tin Woodman tapped Pretense-Wizard on the shoulder. "I don't have the heart to ask you, but you don't by any chance have it in your heart to spare a heart for me?"

"Possibly," said Pretense-Wizard. "Once I figure out what you just said."

"Oh, thank you!" Tin Woodman nearly shed a tear of joy but stopped himself just in time.

"However, it will be broken," said Pretense-Wizard. "A heavy heart or a broken heart is about all you can expect from any heart in this cruel world. I see more advantages in not having a heart. A cold-blooded, heartless man without a care in the world makes for a more confident, determined, although ruthless, man. Much more so than someone who has a heart that can be shattered to pieces."

"Yet, if you are not heartless... I mean, not lacking a heart..." Tin Woodman, regrouping his thoughts, tapped his tin chest with his finger. "If you have the heart to give, I will gladly take it so that I may fill this empty void and forever hold it dear to my heart. Once I get one. A heart, that is."

"Tomorrow."

Dorothy wagged her finger at Pretense-Wizard and snarled, "Toto and I demand that you get us home to Kansas."

"Kansas," Pretense-Wizard gave out a heavy sigh. "There isn't anywhere else you'd rather be? The Himalayas or the Gobi Desert? Someplace of interest and a little more colorful?"

Dorothy shook her head with determination. "Nope. Kansas."

Pretense-Wizard looked at me and, if I could, I would have shrugged my shoulders, indifferently.

Pretense-Wizard thought a long moment. "If none of you reveals my secret, I will do my best to grant your wishes. In the meantime, you will have command of the palace, and all will wait hand, foot, and paw on each of you."

BRAINS, A HEART, THE COURAGE

In the morning, everyone gathered in Dorothy's room where Scarecrow provided us with a soft shoe dance flaunting his excitement.

"Brains, brains, brains," he sang merrily. "Today I will be full of them!"

"We know you will ruff-ruff-ruff," we responded, wishing him well.

"Toto, would you like to accompany me while I get stuffed with brains?" ask Scarecrow.

"Ruff," I agreed.

This I had to see.

When Scarecrow and I entered the Throne Room, we found Pretense-Wizard at a table deep in thought.

"Please, sit down," said Pretense-Wizard.

Scarecrow was happy to do whatever it took to receive his brains and plopped himself down in a chair, his painted face smiling with glee.

"Hold still," said Pretense-Wizard, putting his hands to the sides of Scarecrow's head. "Allow me to take your head from you." With little effort, Pretense-Wizard yanked off his head. He turned and carried his head to the back room.

As Pretense-Wizard disappeared behind a door, he left it slightly ajar. A moment later, I heard the sounds of hammering, sawing, banging, clanking, zipping, stirring, and pouring.

While Pretense-Wizard remained busy in the back room, I glanced up at the headless Scarecrow. Now and again, his hand reached up and searched about, over his shoulders, for his head. Finding that it had not returned, his shoulders would shrug, and he would settle his hand on the arm of the chair and tap his fingers lightly and softly as he waited.

Left with the dull company of a headless Scarecrow, I turned my attention to what Pretense-Wizard was up to in the back room. Deciding to investigate, I trotted to the door, but before I entered, Pretense-Wizard emerged with Scarecrow's head in his hands and marched right past me over to Scarecrow.

"Bran-new," said Pretense-Wizard. Before he replaced Scarecrow's head, he stuck his hand into it, made some adjustments, then wiped off something his hand had collected, smearing it across his pant leg. "Bran-nificent," he declared. "Bran-new brains." Plopping the head onto Scarecrow's neck, he added, "You're bran-ed for life with brains."

Odd, I thought, seeing shiny, pointy things sticking out of Scarecrow's head. Sniffing, I got a whiff of something coming from him that I had smelled before. Something vaguely familiar.

"Well," Scarecrow beamed, "I certainly do feel bright and clever now. I can't wait to impress my friends with my knowledgeable knowledge. Do you have time for the others?"

"Send Tin Woodman in," smiled Pretense-Wizard, rubbing his hands together.

Scarecrow tapped his temple with his finger, "Now that I have the ability to think, I do not think I have to think this request over for my brand new brains tell me it is a no-brainer." He then spun around and sauntered out the door with all sorts of things filling his head.

While Pretense-Wizard stood at the door, watching Scarecrow off, I decided to peek into the back room. I hopped up onto a chair, and then onto the table. There I found coils of wire, long, sharp needles, an assortment of tools in a canvas bag, a jug of water, and a bowl with a wooden ladle sticking out of it. Sniffing at the side of the bag, I swore I could smell the odor of bran. Then, looking over at the bowl, the same odor permeated from it. That deceitful ol' coot had mixed water and bran and had stuffed Scarecrow's head with this mixture, along with coiled wire and needles to give substance and reinforcement. I wanted to expose this fraud to Dorothy so I immediately jumped off the table and dashed out the door, but Scarecow managed to get back to Dorothy and the others before me.

"You would not believe what is on my mind," Scarecrow beamed, promenading spiritedly into Dorothy's room.

"Your head does look different," said Dorothy, with a look of bafflement. "Fuller and prickly, especially with all those needles jutting out of it."

"I think he looks sharp," said Tin Woodman, delighted.

"Sharp as a pin," Lion agreed, appraising him.

Pinhead is how I assessed Scarecrow. However, I decided to remain quiet since divulging the truth would not alter the fact that Scarecrow was no different from before. Without realizing it, he was at times clever and resourceful, but at least now, he could think things through with confidence.

"Well, I'm off to see the Wizard," said Tin Woodman, clanking out of the room. Curious as to what Pretense-Wizard had up his sleeve this time, I decided to trot along back to the Throne Room.

"If you have the heart to give me I will certainly return your kindness with a heartfelt thank you," said Tin Woodman, as we entered the Throne Room.

"I will only have to make a small incision," replied Pretense-Wizard, searching a toolbox and pulling out a small, handheld torch. He lit the end of it with a match, producing a thin, blue flame. He tapped a finger against Tin Woodman's side. "Please raise your arm, if you don't mind."

"As long as you patch it afterward. I would not want to feel a draft."

With the small torch, Pretense-Wizard cut a square from Tin Woodman's side breastplate big enough to stick his fist through. He then reached into his pocket and took out a soft, bright red heart-shaped pin cushion. Attaching a hook to the top of the cushion, he inserted it into Tin Woodman's side and hung it. Then, with a square piece of tin, he covered the hole and soldered it into place.

Having to hold up his left arm for Pretense-Wizard to do his work, Tin Woodman could not see what Pretense-Wizard had inserted into his cavity. "It is a kind heart, is it not?" he asked, lowering his arm and feeling his breastplate with his right hand. "I would not want a coldhearted heart."

"A very soft heart," Pretense-Wizard assured him as he walked Tin Woodman to the door. "The softest anyone could ask for. Now ask Lion to come."

Tin Woodman pounded his breast wholeheartedly as we returned to the others. "What kindness can I do for you?" he asked with a soft sigh.

"You can kindly get out of my way," said Lion, "For it is my turn to get my courage."

"Most heartily," said Tin Woodman, moving aside.

As Lion headed to the Throne Room, Dorothy put her ear to Tin Woodman's breast, and then stood back, a curious look on her face. "I can't hear your heart at all."

"That is because it is such a soft heart," Tin Woodman explained, "So soft that it even softens its beating sound."

"If it is that soft," said Scarecrow, putting his mind to the matter, "it will not easily break."

I trotted off after Lion. As we reached the Throne Room, he held his head high, appearing confident and fearless as he prepared to collect his courage.

"If you have the brains to give Scarecrow and the heart to give Tin Woodman then surely you have the courage to give me," Lion demanded of Pretense-Wizard with a soft growl.

"I most certainly do," said Pretense-Wizard. "Please sit while I get it for you."

I sat next to Lion, eyeing Pretense-Wizard suspiciously as he disappeared into the back room. I could hear the sound of a wooden stool scraping the floor, and then the doors of a high cupboard opening, and closing. A moment later, the sound of liquid pouring into a dish emitted from the back room.

"Here we are," said Pretense-Wizard, returning with a soup bowl filled with some sort of liquid.

Lion sniffed at it as Pretense-Wizard placed it on the floor in front of him. "It is not a pleasant smell," he said. "What is it?"

"A bowl of courage," said Pretense-Wizard. "To gain courage, you must accept courage as it is and drink it. A foul taste is a small price to pay."

Lion raised an eyebrow, grimaced, but then lapped with his wide tongue until the bowl was dry. After a thunderous burp, he smacked his lips and roared furiously, nearly toppling Pretense-Wizard over with his breath. "I feel courageous already, so don't let anyone stand in my way for I fear no one." With that, he turned and strutted out the door with his head and tail held high.

Once Lion was out of sight, Pretense-Wizard turned to me and said, "Can you believe those three? It was a bunch of hooey, hokum, and nonsense, but they accepted it all as though it was real. As though I was a true wizard performing magic."

Why was he confessing this to me? What does he think I am, a dumb dog? Doesn't he realize I can return to my companions any moment and expose him, telling them that what Pretense-Wizard provided was nothing more than humbug? He's just a charlatan. A trickster. However, I decided to remain silent. I was not about to dampen the spirits of my friends by revealing the truth behind what they so desperately wanted. For better or worse, what Pretense-Wizard provided was faith in themselves to be what and whom they wanted to be and I couldn't argue with that.

BALLOON MASTERY

When Dorothy took her turn, she found the door to the Throne Room locked and Soldier guarding it.

"He will summon you when the time comes," said Soldier. He offered no other explanation.

Dorothy, a bit peeved, stomped back to her room with me trotting after her.

Three days went by without a word from Pretense-Wizard and Dorothy felt more and more despondent.

"My heart goes out to you," sniffed Tin Woodman, "but the Wizard soldered it closed and I cannot retrieve it. Here," he handed Dorothy a towel and the oilcan inlaid with precious jewels. "Wipe my tears and oil my joints so I do not rust after shedding heartfelt tears for your predicament."

Scarecrow sat with his gloved fists to the sides of his head and thought hard. "I have much on my mind yet I cannot come up with anything useful to help you, Dorothy. I'm afraid I'm stumped."

Lion moaned, "I wish I could share my courage with you, Dorothy, so that you can be brave while you wait for what may be in store for you."

"You're a lot of help," sighed Dorothy, glumly. "All of you. Thank you."

"You're welcome," Tin Woodman, Lion, and Scarecrow replied.

"Humph!" Dorothy added with an appreciative smile.

I, too, was dispirited and unable to brighten Dorothy's spirits. All any of us could do was wait. Wait and see.

Then, on the fourth day, Girl came to Dorothy and said, "The Great Wizard will see you now."

Dorothy sprang to her feet, and I trotted close behind her, as she dashed to the Throne Room.

"Well...?" Dorothy folded her arms over her chest, one eyebrow raised and tapping her dainty foot as she glared at Pretense-Wizard. "You have something for me?"

Tap-tap-tap!

"I've put much thought into this matter," began Pretense-Wizard.

Tap-tap-tap!

"Only now has the solution come to me."

Tap-tap-tap!

"Please stop that confounded tapping and give me a chance to think with a clear head."

Tap! Silence. Glare!

"Thank you," Pretense-Wizard sighed. "Now, where was I? Oh, yes, the solution. Since you arrived by air in your farmhouse, it seems only logical that is how you should return to Kansas. However, I cannot summon a cyclone to raise your farmhouse, but what I can do is make a balloon similar to the one that brought me here."

"Fair enough," Dorothy considered.

"It was a circus, not a fair, that I came from," corrected Pretense-Wizard. "A circus in Omaha."

"Omaha. Oh, you poor thing," said Dorothy, sympathetically. "No wonder you left."

"It wasn't my idea to leave Omaha," continued Pretense-Wizard. "You see, I was a clown in a very small circus. The circus was so small, that each of us had multiple jobs to carry out. Besides performing as a clown, one of my chores was giving people rides in the basket of this enormous balloon. One day, while I stood in the basket and heated the air to inflate the balloon it unexpectedly broke free of its tether, and up and up I went. The winds were strong and I found I could not control the balloon. When I finally did manage to gain control of the balloon, the only place I found to land was here, in Emerald City. The people, never having seen a balloon or a clown, for that matter, believed me to be a great sorcerer from the heavens and asked if I was a good Witch or a bad Witch. Once they explained about the two wholesome Witches and the two mean-spirited, vengeful Witches they already had, I decided to play it safe and declared myself a Wizard. When asked what are Wizard's talents, I quickly came up with the idea that I can change my appearance at any time. It just so happened that I had my bag with extra clown costumes and makeup with me. Ducking back down into the basket, I changed my makeup, then added a few extra accessories; a bigger nose, floppy ears, large glasses, and a funny hat, and stuffed my clothes with towels to add weight to my body. When I reappeared, the people gasped in awe. I'm also a ventriloquist, so I spoke in a different voice without moving my lips. The people of Emerald City were so impressed that I soon had all at my command."

"Yeah, yeah," grumbled Dorothy, unimpressed. "So what do you need to make a balloon large enough to carry me and Toto out of here?"

"Silk to be cut into a balloon shape," said Pretense-Wizard. "Most importantly, we need glue to cover the outside of the balloon."

"What's the glue for?" puzzled Dorothy.

"For the balloon to rise, we need to inflate it with hot air by building a small fire under it," explained Pretense-Wizard. "The glue is used to keep the air from seeping out. Once we attach a woven basket big enough for us to ride in, off we go."

"Us?" Dorothy raised the other eyebrow. With both eyebrows now raised, she had a surprised look on her face.

Pretense-Wizard sighed. "You have found me out so I know it will only be a matter of time before the citizens of the Emerald City also find me out and string me up to the tallest emerald pole. Therefore, I think it best to get out of here and back to Omaha while I'm still alive."

"You are so fearful of the citizens of the Emerald City that you are willing to return to Omaha?" Dorothy sighed compassionately. "Then, do come along."

"I'll see you off in Kansas first," said Pretense-Wizard. "Then on to, gulp, Omaha."

"That's the spirit," Dorothy smiled and laid a soft punch with her dainty fist across Pretense-Wizard's chin. "Now what?"

"Sew."

"So what?" Dorothy shrugged.

"Sew the balloon together."

"You and me?"

"Not together-together. You sew while I cut out."

"You're leaving?"

"I cut out the fabric while you sew the pieces together to form a balloon."

"Oh," said Dorothy, perplexed for a moment. Then, smiling, she said, "I think I'm getting it now. You intend to cut pieces of fabric and you want me to stitch them together to form a balloon."

Pretense-Wizard slapped his open palm on his forehead in frustration. "Stitch, sew, whatever! Can you do it?"

"Do what?"

"Sew."

"So what?" Dorothy shrugged again.

Pretense-Wizard raised his hands to grab Dorothy by the throat and strangle her, but she poked him playfully in the ribs with her finger.

"Gotcha!" she winked.

That Dorothy! She makes me laugh.

Anyway, over the next three days, Dorothy sewed while Pretense-Wizard cut fabric. I helped by snapping off the ends of the thread with my teeth or pulling the fabric into place. It was hard work, but when Pretense-Wizard brushed the last of the glue over the completed balloon, we were amazed by how professional and functional it looked.

"I now need to inform the people of the Emerald City I will be traveling with you for a short visit outside of Oz," explained the Pretense-Wizard. "I will instruct the citizens that, in my absence, they are to obey Scarecrow for he will be in charge now that he has his wits about him."

Once Scarecrow was informed he would be in charge during Pretense-Wizard's absence, he was in awe that he could now use his brains to command the citizens of the Emerald City. He set off immediately to hone his skill at ordering the citizens to do whatever came to mind, even though, at times, it was a bit bizarre or made no sense at all. Still, the citizens of the Emerald City went along since they were rather a witless bunch and knew no better.

A BUNCH OF HOT AIR

With the balloon completed, Scarecrow, Tin Woodman, and Lion joined the citizens of Emerald City to watch the launch. As a kettle with hot coals, attached to the opening at the bottom of the balloon, heated the air within, the balloon rose high overhead. Dorothy held me as we climbed into the woven basket we will ride in. Pretense-Wizard was already there, disguised in a terrifying Kalidahs costume to hide his true identity in the event something went wrong and he would have to remain in the Land of Oz. The showman that he was, he could not help himself and proceeded into a long and boring farewell speech to the large gathering assembled before us.

As the speech dragged on, the balloon, ever-expanding with hot air, tugged and tugged at the ropes that tethered the balloon to the ground, stretching them to their limits, but Pretense-Wizard could not find an ending to his speech and went on and on, contributing his hot air to the expanse of the balloon.

Dorothy, yawning with every word Pretense-Wizard inflicted upon the poor citizens of Emerald City, suddenly spied a sign on a window of a souvenir shop below. The sign read, "All things emerald, 50% off." Seeing this, Dorothy's eyes lit up like bright luminous bulbs. "Sale!" she squealed. "I haven't gotten anything to take back to Aunt Em and Uncle Henry. Toto, I'm sure you'd want to get some things for your animal friends on the farm."

Before I knew it, she cradled me under her arm, climbed out of the basket, slid down the rope, and hit the ground running toward the emerald shop.

Dumbfounded, Tin Woodman, Scarecrow, and Lion cried out, "Where... where are you going?"

"Shopping," hollered Dorothy over her shoulder. "I'll be back in a second."

Just as we reached the door to the souvenir store, we heard a tremendous gasp from the crowd behind us. When we turned and looked back, we saw that the balloon had broken free of its tether and it was now rising slowly skyward. Pretense-Wizard, continuing with his speech, seemed to take little notice that he was sailing up and away all alone, leaving the citizens of Emerald City craning their necks and straining to hear his fading words.

"Ah, cornhusks!" Dorothy said as Pretense-Wizard and the balloon shrank to little more than specks against a cloudless sky. "Cornhusks!" Dorothy could not think of anything else to say and, cradled under her arm, I was left dumbfounded, but not all that disappointed.

PHIFFT!

I sat with Dorothy on the steps in front of the store as Tin Woodman, Scarecrow and Lion gathered around us, looking confused.

Scarecrow asked, "What's up?"

"Pretense-Wizard," Dorothy snarled, pointing skyward. "That's who."

Dorothy sulked back to her room with me trotting next to her. Scarecrow, Tin Woodman, and Lion followed close behind.

We all watched as Dorothy sat on her bed looking glum. "Phifft!" she said. "Blew my chance." She blew out the side of her mouth at the hair dangling over her cheek. Then her face brightened. "However, I did get some lovely gifts." She held up her basket now filled with an assortment of emerald souvenirs.

"Very nice," Lion agreed. "So how will you get them to Kansas?"

"Phifft!" Dorothy spat sullenly.

"My heart goes out to you," said Tin Woodman, pressing his tin fists over his chest, trying not to cry. "If my heart were not so soft it would be broken."

"Be brave like me." Lion let out a fearsome growl, with an added, "G-r-r-r-r," as though he could instill bravery into her by will.

"Let me put my mind to this matter and see what solution I can attain," said Scarecrow, thinking hard. After a long moment, he threw his hands up in the air and sighed, "Sorry. Not a thing. Perhaps tomorrow," he suggested, with little hope.

Rightfully they were concerned about Dorothy's feelings, although they could have included me. Since my only concern was to be with Dorothy wherever she was, I shrugged it off.

"Phifft!," Dorothy repeated.

Not wanting to mope about like everyone else, I made up my mind to resolve this seemingly irresolvable situation and sniffed about Dorothy's room until I came upon the Golden Cap. Picking it up in my mouth, I carried it to Dorothy and deposited it in front of her. After a few good barks that explained how she could summon the winged monkeys to fly us out of Oz and back to Kansas, Dorothy picked up the cap, patted me on the head, and turned to the others.

"Winged Monkeys," she said with a look of sudden inspiration as though she had just thought of it herself. "I'll use the Golden Cap to summon the winged monkeys so that they can fly Toto and me to Kansas."

I slumped to the floor, tilted my head, and looked up at Dorothy, thinking that people have an annoying way of rephrasing whatever we dogs tell them and then acting as though they came up with it all on their own.

Dorothy decided the Throne Room was the best place to wait for the winged monkeys and we all followed her there. We gathered in a circle at the center of the Throne Room and watched as Dorothy hopped around on one foot, and then the other while muttering the words from the Golden Cap. It was a long wait, but at last, the leader of the winged monkeys arrived and entered.

"You muttered," he said, bowing before her.

"Leader of the winged monkeys," commanded Dorothy, "fly Toto and me to Kansas."

"No can do," said the leader of the winged monkeys. "Even if we knew where Kansas was, we are not allowed to cross over the border of Oz, wherever that may be. Therefore, this command is not permissible."

"Phifft! Ruff!" we all grumbled as the leader of the winged monkeys turned and flew the coop.

"That was certainly a waste of a charm," Dorothy sighed.

"Leaves you with only one left," Tin Woodman nodded sadly.

"Now what are you going to do?" wondered Lion.

"Think about it!" declared Scarecrow. There was a rolling of eyes from each of us as Scarecrow put his mind to figuring out the next course of action. He scrunched his painted face as he thought and thought and his head seemed to grow to the bursting point before he exhausted himself and flopped to the floor. As Tin Woodman and Dorothy raised him to his feet, he said, "I've got it!" We all stared in anticipation for a long moment before he declared with confidence, "Let's rename Emerald City and call it Kansas! Then Dorothy and Toto will not have to leave because they'll already be home."

When the leader of the winged monkeys departed, he had left the door to the Throne Room slightly ajar, and out in the hall I caught sight of Soldier and wondered to myself if he could be of any use to us. Thinking he might, I trotted out and barked at him to follow me. However, it took several stops, looking back at him while repeating my barking request, before he agreed to come along.

Soldier tiptoed into the Throne Room close behind me, looking apprehensively in all directions. "I never know what to expect when I enter the Throne Room," he whispered fretfully.

When Scarecrow saw him, he said brightly, "I have an even more brilliant idea. Let's ask Soldier for help." Scarecrow sauntered up to Soldier and demanded, "Soldier, as your ruler, I demand that you help us get Dorothy and Toto to Kansas."

Soldier looked hesitantly around and then said, "You could try asking a Witch to assist you."

"I've killed the Witches of the East and West and the Good Witch of the North sent us here to get help from the Wizard of Oz," explained

Dorothy, and then added sarcastically, "A big help he turned out to be. He's gone with the wind and I'm still here."

"Have you tried Witch Glinda?" asked Soldier.

"Never heard of her ruff-ruff-ruff," we all replied.

"Few have, but, if I am not mistaken, having few visitors has left her with many unused charms. Possibly she can combine some charms to get you to this Kansas place."

Lion roared, "Dorothy only needs to know in which direction she must travel."

Tin Woodman asked Dorothy, "In which direction haven't we been?"

Before Dorothy had a chance to respond, Scarecrow spoke up. "Let's see. Dorothy has flattened the Wicked Witch of the East so she must have started from there. Then she dissolved the Wicked Witch of the West so it couldn't be in that direction. North?"

"I just said the Good Witch of the North sent me here," said Dorothy, "and I don't believe her name was Glinda."

Scarecrow quickly dismissed north, but continued to think deeply on the subject."

"You're getting close ruff-ruff-ruff," each of us encouraged him.

Scarecrow, snapping his soft fingers, producing no sound, suddenly declared, "South!"

Impressed with Scarecrow's deduction, Tin Woodman turned to Soldier and said, "Tell us how Dorothy and Toto may get there."

Soldier gulped and whispered unsurely, "Head south?"

"A practical solution," confirmed Scarecrow. "We'll send Dorothy and Toto south this instant."

"However, Your Braininess," Soldier advised with cautious hesitation, "to reach Good Witch Glinda one must cross a vast forest, a perilous desert, and who knows what's beyond that. It will be especially dangerous for a petite girl, and her furry, helpless companion."

I looked around wondering whom Soldier referred to as helpless. Possibly Lion because he was the only other one besides me that was furry. Still, he had been of some use on our journey so I would not consider him helpless. And why would Dorothy take Lion along and not me? Considering in the Land of Oz anything was possible and implausibly plausible, we may have, unbeknownst to me, switched roles, and it was now Lion's turn to be human's best friend while I remained behind to be King of Beasts. Not a bad turn of events as far as I was concerned.

"Do not fear," roared Lion.

I looked over at him and saw him sitting up, his back straight, and stretching his head high into the air.

"I fear nothing and I will protect Dorothy."

There, I knew it. We did switch roles. I'm now King of Beasts!

Tin Woodman, leaning heavily on the handle of his ax, said, "If there is a forest, you'll need me to whack it and lay it to waste."

My ears perked up excitedly. Trees. Squirrels, perhaps. Even if I had switched roles with Lion, I was not about to miss out if there were trees and squirrels involved so, I too, was determined to go along and wagged my tail and barked my decision excitedly.

Dorothy picked me up and held me in her arms, rubbing my head in gratitude, then spoke to Lion. "It is courageous of you, Lion, to choose to accompany me and Toto as we attempt again to find our way to Kansas."

What? Wait! Did our roles reverse, and I'm back again, merely being Dorothy's companion? My tail stopped wagging and I slumped my head on her arm. So much for being King of Beasts.

"I am also grateful to you, Tin Woodman, for having it in your heart to be there if trees need to be whacked to smithereens." She patted Lion on the snout and kissed Tin Woodman on his tin cheek.

"I suppose we best get going," Scarecrow announced with swagger.

"You want to leave the Emerald City and come with us, too?" asked Dorothy, surprised, but pleased.

"Of course," said Scarecrow. "It is you who pulled me off the pole in the field which allowed me to have my head filled with all sorts of stuff. It is only natural that I come along and do the thinking for all of you with all the brains I have."

"You're so full of it ruff-ruff-ruff," we all cheered.

Once we had rested and collected everything we needed, we asked Girl to safeguard the gold gifts the Winkies had presented to us. Being of solid gold, they would weigh us down. After Tin Woodman selected an ax with a wood handle, we thanked Soldier and Girl and marched off to the front gate. Gate Guardian met us there with a look of surprise that seemed to be his recurring expression.

"You're not thinking of going back out into the dangerous world, are you?" he asked with a look of astonishment, which was a slight variation from his typical facial expression.

"Think we are afraid of the unknown?" Lion spoke courageously.

"It will warm my heart to be there when Dorothy sets off to her beloved Kansas," said Tin Woodman wholeheartedly.

"I think, therefore I am," said Scarecrow, after much thought.

Gate Guardian asked him, "Will you return to rule over us? We are a bit witless without a ruler."

"I shall think the matter through thoroughly," replied Scarecrow, mulling it over thoughtfully. "Though, do not despair for I am certain I will conclude that I will best serve the world by ruling over you witless people until all of you become as witty as I am."

With that unsettling thought, Gate Guardian unlocked our glasses and off we skipped, ambled, trotted, and clunked southward.

UNRULY FOREST

It was late in the afternoon when we came upon the vast forest Soldier mentioned. The forest was much too vast to go around and so dense that we had difficulty trying to locate an entrance.

Tin Woodman stepped forward. "Shall I whack it to smithereens?"

"Not necessary." Scarecrow pointed to a narrow path between two enormous oaks. "Through here." He ambled forward and we followed in line into the narrow opening. Then, without warning, a branch of one tree swung down and smacked Scarecrow straight on, knocking him back against us, and we all fell like dominos, one on the other. Well, except for me, since I stood well below the branch's forceful swipe.

With everyone flat on their back, I gritted my teeth, growled, then charged at the offending tree. I barked and barked at its bark and clamped my teeth on it so the tree could feel that my bite was worse than my bark. The tree's limbs swung down but missed me entirely since I kept low to the ground as always. I snapped, barked, bit, and growled menacingly, frustrating the tree to no end.

Scarecrow, jumping to his feet, contemplated the discourteous tree.

"Enough, Toto," he said to me. "You'll only get splinters of bark between your teeth." Turning to the others, he said, "I suspect we better leave this tree be and go around it."

As Scarecrow attempted to bypass the discourteous tree by going to the other side of its neighboring tree, the companion tree swung its branch and slapped Scarecrow on his painted face and he soared through the air behind us.

"Ah-ha! A genus of unfavorable nature this entire forest must be," Scarecrow cried out, his body crumpled into a pile with only his painted face visible. Dorothy, after helping Tin Woodman and Lion to their feet and paws, collected the straw scattered about, and re-stuffed Scarecrow.

"What are we to do if these trees do not want us to go through to the other side?" asked Dorothy, helping Scarecrow to his feet.

"Make like a tree and leave?" suggested Scarecrow.

"Which way?" asked Lion.

"That way," Scarecrow pointed in the direction we came from.

"That will not do," said Dorothy. "I must go through this forest by any means if I am to reach the castle of the Witch Glinda."

"Of all those means, which one do you suggest we try first?" ask Tin Woodman.

Scarecrow thought for a long moment. "I know. Let's make a run for it." With that, he pretended to roll back his sleeves and took one determined step back. Then, with a burst of speed, he charged headlong between the two offending trees. Unfortunately, both trees seized him with their limbs, tore him apart, and flung the parts over our heads again. Dorothy looked back at Scarecrow, shrugged, dismayed, then dashed back to retrieve his parts and reassemble him.

"You need to learn to pull yourself together," she said to Scarecrow, reconnecting his parts. "I will not always be around to rescue you."

Lion said, "It was a courageous attempt by Scarecrow, but he is too soft in body and mind to tackle these trees and I don't believe my roar and fearlessness will be of use to uproot them. This, Tin Woodman, is your specialty."

Scarecrow shouted, "That's right, Tin Woodman. Exfoliate and graft with your ax those ill-mannered hybrids, limb from limb, until they are nothing but kindling!"

Tin Woodman, with a heartfelt sigh, tapped his ax on the open palm of his hand. "It warms my heart, now that I have a heart to warm, to know I can proceed wholeheartedly to splinter these timbers into tiny toothpicks."

Tin Woodman slid one hand up one arm, and then switched to the other arm, as though he was rolling up sleeves that he lacked. Then he marched boldly up to the unruly trees. Alarmed, the branches of both trees shot upwards, quivering, but not high enough to evade the swing of his ax. With each swing, branches fell to the ground one after another until the offending trees were limbless trunks.

"Good work!" exalted Scarecrow as he bounded to his feet and came up to Tin Woodman and patted him softly on the shoulder.

"Fortunately, I am no longer heartless," replied Tin Woodman, pressing his hand over where he thought his heart rested within his tin chest. "If I were without a heart I would not have the heart to seek vengeance on your behalf and whack these trees warm-heartedly."

"You have successfully bared these two unruly trees and left them standing divested, denuded, and au natural..." Scarecrow said. Dorothy, upon hearing Scarecrow's description, gasped and blushed, and turned her eyes away as any proper young girl might do. "However," continued Scarecrow, "we have the rest of the forest to contend with. This will surely slow us down if we are to raze this entire forest."

"I don't think that will be necessary," Tin Woodman assured him, tapping the handle of his ax on his tin hand as he sinisterly eyed the trees that remained in their path. Fearful of Tin Woodman's ax, the trees parted, providing a clear and wide path to the other side.

As we now traveled untroubled through the forest, Dorothy said, "I have never seen a forest so rude as this one."

Scarecrow took little time drawing a thoughtful inference. "Possibly this forest has a deep-rooted resentment for those with axes to grind and those who accompany them. Or the forest may be too dense to understand we meant them no harm and we have every right to lumber through it. Whatever their motive, their actions lack fertile merit and were ungrounded."

"Ruff," I praised him since, in my opinion, Scarecrow did not appear to be barking up the wrong tree in his appraisal.

PORCELAIN WORLD

Coming out of the forest, we came upon an extremely high, smooth, and lustrous white wall that stretched to the east and west as far as the eye could see.

Dorothy ran her hand over its smooth pearly surface. "China," she marveled.

"The Great Wall of China," Scarecrow announced, impressed, "yet it doesn't seem that we have traveled as far."

"No," corrected Dorothy. "I meant it is made of china as in porcelain china."

Scarecrow continued, apparently not having heard Dorothy. "A cow, crossing the field I once guarded, mentioned that having jumped over the moon, she saw this great wall from outer space. However, not having even half a mind at the time, I disregarded her claim."

Dorothy, wanting to return to the matter at hand, lamented, "It is too high and smooth to scale and who knows how long it will take to go around it? Even if it is possible to reach one end or the other."

Lion peered toward the top of the wall. "This wall is much greater than my ability to leap and I fear anyone riding me will fall back to their demise if I cannot soar over it."

Tin Woodman, gauging the density of the wall's surface, concluded, "It will only dull my blade if I attempt to hack through it, and who knows how thick this wall is."

Scarecrow, having another brainstorm, concluded, "In my very knowledgeable opinion, I think it best that we turn around and go back and forget about this whole Kansas thing entirely."

Dorothy, though saddened, had to agree with Scarecrow that this wall was too challenging of an obstacle to overcome, but I thought differently. Seeing Tin Woodman's ax hanging at his side and knowing that the forest abounded with timber behind us, I clamped my teeth onto the blunt end of the ax and backed my way toward the forest pulling Tin Woodman with me.

Lion sighed. "Even Toto has given up hope and wants to return."

I let go of Tin Woodman's ax and barked, "With Tin Woodman's ax and the forest of timber we can construct a means to scale the wall." I waited for a response to my suggestion, but realizing it was not coming, I barked, "Let me demonstrate." I turned and ran back into the woods. There I found a small branch and, grasping it in my mouth, I ran back with it and placed it at the base of the wall. "See?" I barked. "Understand now?" They each looked down at me and shrugged. Since this was a common response they usually give me when I'm trying to explain something to them, I knew I better not waste any more time reiterating my suggestion verbally, so I continued with my visual demonstration. Without another word, I ran back into the forest, collected two more branches, and deposited them on the first. It was only when I stepped up on the mound of branches, where I was elevated, did Scarecrow understand.

"That's a thought," said Scarecrow. "Let's have Tin Woodman chop down the entire forest and then we can pile all the branches and trunks up against the wall. Once we have finished we should be able to walk up and over it."

Tin Woodman, looking back at the forest, said, "What if I just chop enough wood to construct a ladder? That would require less time."

"Very thoughtful of you," Scarecrow agreed. "And efficient."

While Tin Woodman chopped wood, Dorothy lay down for a nap, and Lion and I curled up next to her for a quick snooze. In the meantime, Scarecrow, never needing sleep, watched Tin Woodman work away without a thought in his head. With the wood ready to assemble, Scarecrow gathered pieces of vine and helped Tin Woodman tie the ladder together.

"Done," announced Tin Woodman sometime later. Dorothy, Lion, and I sprang to our feet instantly, fully alert, and ready to go. "Who's first?"

"That would be me," said Dorothy, quickly scaling the ladder. "Ladies first, you know." Once she reached the top, she sat down and said, "Oh my," as she looked into the other side. I was next and when I reached the top I could not help but bark, "Oh my," when I saw what had impressed Dorothy. One after the other, Tin Woodman, Scarecrow, and Lion scaled the ladder to the top of the wall and, the first words out of their mouths as they sat down on the ledge, were, "Oh my."

"It's a porcelain world," Dorothy remarked, awestruck. "The houses, people, and animals are all made of porcelain china. Even the ground looks like a large porcelain china dish."

Out of the corner of my eye, I caught sight of an egg-shaped porcelain man teetering on the wall some distance away. He suddenly lost his balance and fell backward into the porcelain world where he smashed into porcelain pieces. Almost instantly, a small porcelain king rushed to the aid of the cracked porcelain egg-man but, even with the help of all of his porcelain horses and all of his porcelain men, they could not put the porcelain egg-man back together again.

Tin Woodman shouted, getting my attention, "Look, a tiny porcelain dairymaid is milking a tiny porcelain cow."

"There," Lion raised his front paw, "That appears to be a tiny porcelain Princess."

Scarecrow frowned, "Why is that tiny porcelain man standing on his head?"

"It must be a porcelain clown," Dorothy said in wonderment. "They are so beautiful, these porcelain creatures."

Ecstatic, Dorothy emptied her basket of all things emerald souvenirs over the forest side of the wall and then gave Scarecrow a solid whack on the back with her hand, tumbling him headfirst off the wall and onto the porcelain surface below where he landed with a soft thump. She then slid down from the wall and dropped onto his midsection. Swoosh! Realizing this did nothing to harm Scarecrow, the rest of us, one after the other, slid off the wall, and we dropped onto Scarecrow to soften our landing.

Once we were all in the porcelain world, Tin Woodman gathered up the straw knocked out of Scarecrow, and stuffed it back in. In the meantime, Dorothy was tiptoeing up behind the tiny porcelain dairymaid and porcelain cow. With one swipe she snatched the dairymaid and, with another the cow, and deposited both in her basket. Having observed this, I dashed up to Dorothy to see what was going on.

From within Dorothy's basket, a tiny, porcelain-like voice grumbled, "What do you think you're doing?"

Dorothy smiled pleasantly into the basket and responded blithely, "You are going to look beautiful on Aunt Em's mantelpiece."

"Who is Aunt Em?" the tiny voice asked from within the basket.

"My aunt who lives in Kansas."

"Oh no!" the voice shrieked. "You cannot take me out of my porcelain world and put me on a mantle. I will harden and never move again."

"I expect that would be the case. It would be awful if you could run away and I am left with no mementos after all the trouble I've been through."

"Think you got trouble," the tiny voice snapped bitterly.

"Hush!" said Dorothy, glancing about for another pretty porcelain item to collect.

"Please let me go so I can remain alive in my porcelain world," cried the dairymaid.

"Moo!" pleaded the cow, expressing the same wish.

Disregarding their pleas, Dorothy covered them with the cloth from her basket and skipped along. Before the porcelain princess and clown knew it, Dorothy was upon them. She snatched them up and deposited them into her basket. After pocketing a few more porcelain occupants of this porcelain world, she turned to our companions coming up behind us.

Brushing her hair back with her fingers and sighing with satisfaction, she announced, "I think I'm through shopping for the day. We can mosey on out of here now."

We continued southward toward the opposite end of the porcelain world looking for a way out. As Dorothy led the way, the tiny porcelain people and creatures in our path scattered like rats in all directions. Many, glancing back at Dorothy, fell, breaking off various parts of their tiny bodies and leaving them behind as they hobbled off to safety.

Scarecrow, observing their mishaps, concluded, "One would think it would best to slow down and not run off haphazardly as they do. These porcelain people appear very delicate and easily broken."

"I must be very careful of my package of porcelain prizes, too," Dorothy agreed, tapping softly the side of her basket with her hand.

Scarecrow pointed at her basket. "Fragile. Handle with care," he recommended.

"I will certainly take your advice into consideration," said Dorothy, holding the handle of the basket carefully with both hands.

"Harmful if swallowed," continued Scarecrow. "Not recommended for children under two years of age. Keep the right side up. Examine contents before accepting..."

When we reached the far end of the porcelain world, we were surprised to find a sturdy porcelain ladder against the wall.

"This is very kindhearted of them," remarked Tin Woodman, "knowing we needed a ladder to scale the wall to the other side."

Scarecrow added, pointing to his bulging pinhead, "They were certainly using their brains, or else we would be stuck in this porcelain world forever."

"Certainly very courageous of them," added Lion, "considering they appeared apprehensive. Yet they place this ladder at our disposal."

"I think they just want us out of here, the sooner the better," was Dorothy's simple explanation.

I certainly agreed with her after observing the porcelain figures fleeing in panic whenever she turned a contemplative, roving eye in their direction.

LION'S KINGDOM

Once on the other side of the porcelain wall, we found ourselves in a lush, tropical forest, but not one as dense as to require Tin Woodman to whack a path through it. However, this forest was much darker and filled with uneasy sounds that came from the shadows all around us.

"Fear not," said Lion, "for this is my kind of forest. I am familiar with all the sounds you hear and it makes me feel very much at home. Come. Follow me closely and no harm will come to you."

Deep within the forest, we came upon a large gathering of wild animals. Tigers, bears, and elephants, to name a few, were in conference, arguing and appearing very uneasy. When they turned and saw Lion, a large tiger excused himself from the gathering and trotted up to him.

"Glad that you have come, my King," Tiger bowed before Lion. Looking at Dorothy and then at me, he said, "I see you've brought lunch and a small appetizer."

"No," said Lion. "These are my friends, Dorothy and Toto."

"Too bad," said Tiger, looking very disappointed, his stomach growling with hunger. "Anyway, we are in dire need of the King of Beasts to spare us from a terrible monster."

"What could be so terrible?" inquired Lion.

"A gigantic, hairy spider with legs as tall as trees with a gluttonous appetite, has been eating everything in sight," said Tiger. "All the animals in this forest are in fear of it, and that goes for yours truly."

"Oh my," gulped Lion. "And you would like me to dispose of this giant spider?"

"No. Just let it go about eating until there is not an animal left in the kingdom," replied Tiger, sarcastically. Then, taking a firmer stance, he said, "Of course we want you to do something about this threat to our lives. You're the King of Beasts, aren't you?"

Lion considered the request a moment and then said, "I will kill this spider only if you and all the other animals of this forest make me your ruler for life."

"I'm sure we'll have no problem with that," said Tiger. "Better that, than finding ourselves spider droppings on the forest landscape."

"Where is this giant spider?"

"In that direction," Tiger lifted his forepaw and pointed.

Lion turned to us and said, "Relax here while I take care of some minor business." He then trotted bravely to where man, girl, dog, tin woodman, or scarecrow have never gone before; a clearing on the other side of a dense grouping of trees. It was not long before we heard a distant swoosh and thud and then we saw Lion trotting back towards us with a smug expression.

"What happened ruff-ruff-ruff?" we asked in wonderment.

"Caught the spider napping," said Lion, his chest bulging with pride. "The spider had a massive body and a massive head with massive jaws, but only a spindly neck connecting his head to his body. Gauging this, I jumped onto its back, and with one swing of my sharp claws, I cut right through his neck and his head dropped with a thud onto the ground."

"Spiders do frighten me," said Dorothy, impressed. "Even tiny ones."

A tiny spider dashed between us unseen by all, but me. With one good whack, I squashed it flat. However, not wanting to upstage Lion in his moment of glory, I kept this valiant deed to myself.

Tiger and all the other animals gathered around Lion. They all agreed that he will forever be their ruler. However, Lion expressed that this must wait until he has seen Dorothy and I off to Kansas.

BUTTHEADS

We were off once more, making our way through the forest. When we came out the other end, we found ourselves faced with a steep hill. It was bare, except for many large boulders scattered all over it and there seemed no way to get around it.

"This will not be a very easy climb," remarked Tin Woodman.

Scarecrow went forward, saying, "We have no choice but to scale this hill if we wish to reach the castle of Good Witch Glinda."

Scarecrow led the way and we followed close behind him.

When Scarecrow reached the first boulder, a small, squat man, with an extremely large head, appeared. The top of his head was flat and was supported by a long neck.

"This is Butthead Hill and we will not let you pass," said the man in a loud, booming voice.

"Ha!" exclaimed Scarecrow, sauntering forward, disregarding the threat. "We will go over this hill and down the other side as we please."

Suddenly, the man's neck stretched and, as though being fired out of a canon, his head flung forward and hit Scarecrow squarely in the midsection, sending him sailing backward over our heads and down toward the bottom of the hill. His straw stuffing flew everywhere as he hit bottom.

"Oh my," cried Dorothy, looking back at the fallen Scarecrow.

"Humph!" said Tin Woodman, angrily banging his tin chest with his ax. "I'll show this butthead that he cannot stop us from crossing this hill."

Unfortunately, as Tin Woodman scampered up the hill, other buttheads appeared from behind large boulders, and they too flung their heads, striking his body on all sides and sending him plummeting down the hill.

"Oh my," cried Dorothy as Tin Woodman clanked and bounced past us.

Lion growled fiercely, "How dare these buttheads strike my friends. I am King of Beasts and these buttheads do not know what they're in for!"

Lion, unfortunately, did not know what he was in for, as he sprinted up the hill where more buttheads suddenly appeared. They stretched their necks and pounded him with their buttheads. With the wind knocked out of him, Lion tumbled past us, like a big, shaggy, furry ball, down the hill.

"Oh my," cried Dorothy, her hands to the sides of her face as she watched Lion cascade to where Scarecrow and Tin Woodman lay at the bottom of the hill in a heap.

Not wanting to be plummeted by buttheads, and having used up her *oh mys*, Dorothy scurried down the hill to aid our fallen comrades. It was now up to me to tackle this hill.

"Ruff!" I barked and snarled as I scurried up the hill, bobbing and weaving this way and that way, easily dodging their butthead attacks.

"Hey, no fair!" the first of the buttheads complained, "This tiny thing is no easy target for our huge buttheads."

Retracting and flinging their heads repeatedly, they continued to miss me and often hit each other with loud thuds, causing them to groan miserably. As their buttheads swayed dizzily over their squat bodies a display of stars circled overhead.

Although I could bypass the buttheads and make it to the other side of the hill, I knew my companions could not. Turning and going back down the hill, I continued to dodge their futile attempts to strike me.

Once safely away from the buttheads, I trotted down to where Dorothy sat next to Scarecrow, packing his straw back into his body.

"They knocked the stuffing out of me," said Scarecrow, not having felt a thing.

Tin Woodman, lying next to Scarecrow, complained, "I have a ringing in my hollow, tin head."

"Answer it," groaned Lion, curled into a ball and his tongue hanging from the side of his mouth. Rubbing his body where the buttheads struck him, he added, "Ooh, that smarts."

Not able to summon up another *oh my* from her restricted repertoire of expressions, Dorothy added, "Whatever shall we do now? We will never make it over this hill with all those buttheads stopping us."

Of course, I knew that meant I had to step forward with a plan to get us home. Noticing that Dorothy was still wearing the Golden Cap, I put my paws on Dorothy's back, snatched the Golden Cap between my teeth, and pulled it from her head.

"Toto!" Dorothy snapped, feeling her head for the missing Golden Cap. "What did you do that for?"

I went around to face Dorothy, dropped it into her lap, and explained in several barks that she still had one more command of the winged monkeys. With that, she could summon them to carry us to the other side.

Dorothy picked up the Golden Cap from her lap with one hand while rubbing my head with the other, appearing to be contemplating my suggestion. Finally, after a very long moment of deliberation, she said to the others, "I've got it. I still have one more shot at commanding the winged monkeys with this Golden Cap. They can carry us over Butthead Hill and take us to the other side."

While hopping on one foot, then the other, Dorothy muttered the charm that changed with each chant. Soon the sky darkened with winged monkeys.

"Again?" questioned the leader of the winged monkeys. "What is your third and final demand, I mean, command?"

"We need a lift," said Dorothy.

"Which way?"

"That way."

Soon we were all sailing high over the Butthead Hill, completely out of reach of the furious, flinging heads below us.

GOOD WITCH GLINDA

As with our first flight, Dorothy sat on the clasped arms of two winged monkeys and I sat within the basket she held on her lap. Soaring high in the air, I looked down at beautiful fields, brooks, and well-paved roads. I marveled at how wonderful it appeared in comparison to Kansas.

Nearing a pretty farmhouse, the winged monkeys swooped down and settled us gently at the front door.

"That's it," said the leader of the winged monkeys. "You've reached your destination. You're done, we're done, and we're out of here." With that, we watched as the leader guided the winged monkeys up, up, and away.

"Hello, there," said a pleasant voice behind us.

We turned to see a squat little woman sweeping the porch of her farmhouse. Dorothy looked at her, her house, and the fence surrounding it. "This must be the land of red," she said, for everything here, including what you wear is red."

"Ruby red," smiled the little lady. "What can I do for you?"

Both Dorothy and I sniffed the air and smelled something delicious from within the farmhouse. "Feed us ruff," we replied together. "We're famished ruff-ruff!"

The little woman looked behind us at the others. "What about your companions?"

"Oh, Scarecrow and Tin Woodman never eat," said Dorothy.

Lion, speaking for himself, asked, "Do you have any farm animals about?"

"In the barn," replied the little woman with a suspicious glance at Lion.

"If you don't mind," said Lion, "I think I'll remain outside and fend for myself."

Dorothy and I entered the farmhouse while Scarecrow and Tin Woodman idled the time away on the porch. Lion, meanwhile, set off by himself.

Dorothy sat at the table and I sat on the floor by the fireplace and we ate our meals. When we had finished, Dorothy rose to leave and I trotted after her.

"We are grateful for the hospitality you have provided us," said Dorothy, thanking the woman for the two of us as we stood on the front porch.

"In the land of the Quadlings, you will find all of us generous and good-natured, just as our Good Witch Glinda is to us all," said the little woman.

"How do we find this Good Witch Glinda?"

"Just take Good Witch Glinda Road south until you reach Good Witch Glinda Body and Repair Shop, which is across from Good Witch Glinda Grocery and Feed, and the Good Witch Glinda Post Office," the little woman advised us. "Then make a sharp left onto Good Witch Glinda Boulevard, and follow it until you reach Good Witch Glinda Castle. Can't miss it since there is a good-sized sign that proclaims, '*Castle of Good Witch Glinda*,' dominating the skyline over it."

"Would the castle be red?"

"Why would you think otherwise?" the little woman frowned.

We saw Lion trotting away from the barn with a contented smile and a large toothpick jutting out of the corner of his mouth. When he reached us, we said our goodbyes and started down Good Witch Glinda Road.

Following the little woman's directions, it was not long before we reached a towering arched gate with "*Good Witch Glinda Gate*" inscribed in the wrought iron framework. Entering, we made our way to the steps of the Good Witch Glinda Castle. There, we were met by three pretty ladies in uniform with badges over their breasts that proclaimed them to be Good Witch Glinda Soldier One, Two, and Three respectively.

"What can we do for you?" the three Good Witch Glinda Soldiers asked in unison.

"We're here to see the Good Witch Glinda of the Good Witch Glinda Castle," said Dorothy. "Is she in?"

"We'll see if she will see you," they replied with a cheerful smile. Then they turned and entered through a large door carved with the words, "*Good Witch Glinda Entrance*" above it.

Scarecrow, looking about as we waited, noticed a sign on the edge of the pavement where a small field of grass grew near the castle wall. The sign read "*Keep off the Good Witch Glinda Grass.*" Next to it was a mailbox with "*Good Witch Glinda Mailbox*" painted on one side. Drawing these to our attention, he remarked, "I would suspect this Good Witch Glinda has an idiosyncrasy with name recognition."

Just then, the three Good Witch Glinda Soldiers returned.

"Good Witch Glinda will see you," they said, "only after you have cleaned up a bit. You do look wretched and some of you have excessive body odor."

Dorothy lifted an arm, smelled her armpit, and grimaced. "Underarm order."

Scarecrow, imitating her actions, said, "Musty corn stalk."

Tin Woodman followed suit. "I need a change of oil."

Lion, breathing in deeply, said, with pride, "I reek of the wild."

Myself, I preferred to keep my nose out of it.

The three Good Witch Glinda Soldiers, waving their hands across their noses said, "We will show you to your rooms."

The Good Witch Glinda Soldiers led Dorothy and I to one room where two other Good Witch Glinda Soldiers in uniform were preparing a bath. Then each of the Good Witch Glinda Soldiers split up to lead Scarecrow, Lion, and Tin Woodman to each of their rooms.

After Dorothy undressed and slipped into the tub, I decided to see what became of my other companions.

In one room, Scarecrow could not help but giggle hysterically with intermittent sighs of delight as Good Witch Glinda Soldier One stuck her soft, delicate hands inside his body and slowly and meticulously rearranged clean straw into a more fitting form.

Trotting over to Tin Woodman's room, I found him lying on his stomach on a large slab. There, he moaned pleasurably as Good Witch Glinda Soldier Two polished and buffed his tin body from the tip of his head to the bottom of his tin feet and everywhere in between with gentle, unhurried, and purposeful rubs of tin polish and cloth.

Entering Lion's room, I found him face down on a thick carpet as Good Witch Glinda Soldier Three groomed his body and mane with a comb in one hand and a brush in the other. With each leisurely and tender stroke of comb and brush, Lion growled blissfully.

As for myself, I could not find any pretty-numeral soldier to take care of me and soon wandered back to Dorothy. By then she was dressed and presentable. Smiling at me, she picked me up and, after one quick whiff, looked back at the tub. However, to my relief, all three Good Witch Glinda Soldiers reappeared at our door beckoning us to follow them.

"Good Witch Glinda will now see you," they chimed in harmony and then turned to lead the way.

With another whiff, Dorothy dropped me to the floor and hurried out. After quickly recovering, I scampered after her, feeling fortunate to have escaped a bath.

OUR COMPANIONS, LEAVING their rooms beaming with deep satisfaction and emitting pleasurable sighs, soon joined us. We all fell in behind the three Good Witch Glinda Soldiers who led us down a long and brightly lit hall. Official portraits, about a few hundred in all, with the likes of the Beautiful Good Witch Glinda lined the walls along the way. We knew these were portraits of Good Witch Glinda because a gilded placard with the words "*Beautiful Good Witch Glinda*," inscribed in bold lettering hung under each one.

"Please come in," Good Witch Glinda invited us into a large room where we found a dozen more official portraits of her hanging on the walls.

"Pleased to meet you, Good Witch Glinda," Dorothy curtsied before her.

"You've heard of me?" Good Witch Glinda smiled, bouncing the curls of her hair with her hand portentously. Sitting up on her high throne, she appeared very beautiful and smiled at each of us with a twinkle in her eyes.

Glancing at the portraits and then at the witch's flowing gown with "*Good Witch Glinda*" embroidered in large letters all over it, Dorothy said simply, "Your name gets around."

"Though you would not believe how few in the Land of Oz know I exist at all," said Good Witch Glinda, her smile tensing, eyes narrowing, and face flushing. "Sure, everyone knows about the bad witches. I mean, they cause so much trouble that their names are on everyone's lips. Then there's that publicity-seeking Good Witch of the North who always, and I mean always, appears at any event or the murder of some old witch just so she can remain in the limelight. Do you see me out there? No! I'm south. Way south. No one thinks about the South. It's always north, east, and west. South is for losers. No one ever wants to visit Good Witch Glinda because she's south."

We could practically see steam issuing from her ears, as her face flushed a deep, ruby red.

"Perhaps," Scarecrow took a stab, "no one goes south because of the menacing trees, fragile porcelain world, giant spiders, and buttheads that are a troublesome barrier."

"So you think that is the reason no one comes to visit?" Good Witch Glinda asked, with hopeful eyes.

We all nodded in agreement, thinking it was logical.

Good Witch Glinda, reassured that her lack of visitation was nothing personal, regained her composure, smiled, and asked, "How, then, may I be of assistance?"

"I'm trying to find my way home," said Dorothy. "Home to Kansas," she clarified. "Is it possible for me to return to Kansas?"

"You could have returned to this Kansas place any time you wished, had you put your mind to it."

"I don't understand," said Dorothy, confused.

Good Witch Glinda pointed her wand at Dorothy's feet. The tip of the wand was so close to me that I was tempted to snap at it, but I held back, not wanting to distract from the ensuing conversation.

"You are wearing the sparkly shoes of the Wicked Witch of the East and she used those to get around the Land of Oz until you flattened her into a pancake."

"You heard about that?" asked Dorothy.

"I have this globe thingy that shows me everything that is going on in the Land of Oz," said Good Witch Glenda. "Although the reception is not always so great. Gets fuzzy at times. I should call for technical support, but I do get tired of being kept on hold and the awful music they play while I'm waiting. It drives me crazy."

Dorothy looked down at the sparkly shoes. "If these shoes can take me home, why didn't the Witch of the North tell me that?"

"I think that, after all these thousands of years, the twirling act that jets her from here to there finally loosened something up here." Good Witch Glinda tapped her finger to her head.

"You mean, I just need to do a quick spin, like the Witch of the North, and that will take me home?"

"I'll explain that in a moment," said Good Witch Glinda, glancing at our companions. "First, who are these things with you, and what do they want?"

After Dorothy made formal introductions, Scarecrow spoke first.

"I only wish to see Dorothy off to Kansas before I return to the Emerald City. I am officially their ruler, you know, now that I have the brains to do it," he pointed to his pinhead head.

Then Tin Woodman stepped forward. "My heart goes out to the Winkies in the West since they have no ruler and so desperately want someone to tell them what to do. I will surely rule them with the kind heart I acquired, once I know Dorothy is on her way."

Lion breathed on the claws of his right paw and then polished them smugly against his chest. "There is a forest of animals in want of someone as courageous as me to rule over their kingdom. I shall return to my forest kingdom once I am confident that Dorothy is on her way home."

Turning back to Dorothy, Good Witch Glinda said, "Say your goodbyes now, then I'll explain how you return to this Kansas place. If that's really where you want to go."

"Your Highness," Dorothy interjected. "For my companions to return to their destinations, there are barriers to consider."

"The barriers you managed to cross?" asked Good Witch Glinda.

Dorothy nodded. "Finding a way back into the Porcelain World may not be too difficult and I'm sure the inhabitants there will do their best to get them out the other side. They weren't too keen on us being there in the first place."

"Mostly you, Dorothy," injected Scarecrow, pointing to the items in her basket.

Without looking down, Dorothy adjusted the cloth over the basket, making sure it was fully covered. With a glance at Scarecrow, she went on. "Since Lion took care of the giant spider and Tin Woodman has command of the unruly forest, I see no problems there. However, that leaves the buttheads of Butthead Hill to overcome."

Good Witch Glinda frowned. "You seemed to have managed to get through."

"It was with the help of the winged monkeys," Dorothy explained. "They flew us over the hill of buttheads, out of their reach. It will be necessary for my friends to return that way, but now I no longer have a charm left in my Golden Cap to summon the winged monkeys. Surely Scarecrow, Tin Woodman, and Lion will be attacked and driven back and will never be able to return to their Kingdom, Castle, or Emerald City."

Good Witch Glinda tapped her fingers on the arm of her throne, thinking. Finally, she shrugged and said, "Too bad. They'll all just have to remain here under the care of my beautiful Good Witch Glinda Soldiers."

Scarecrow, Tin Woodman, and Lion eyed each other with broad smiles on their faces. By the looks in their eyes, I imagined them considering staying right where they were. However, I knew that it would better serve the Land of Oz if each returned to those who so desperately needed them. Thinking fast, it occurred to me that the Good Witch Glinda could take over the Golden Cap and summon the winged monkeys for air travel and I barked this suggestion to Dorothy and the others, but do you think anyone listened? No! They were too busy trying to hush me as though I was interrupting their thoughts. Frustrated, I decided to take immediate action. I turned and got up on my hind legs with my front paws high up on Dorothy's leg, craning my neck up toward the Golden Cap. However, Dorothy mistook my intentions and scolded me.

"Down, Toto, down." She shook her leg, and waved her finger. "That is not nice at all. You're embarrassing me."

Still, I persisted and Dorothy found it necessary to bend down and pull me away. As she bent over, the Golden Cap slipped from her head and fell to the floor. I immediately turned to it, snapped it up in my mouth, and then sprang up into the lap of the Good Witch Glinda.

"Pesky little creature," she said, horrified, reluctant to touch me.

I dropped the Golden Cap on her lap and barked, "There's a charm in the cap. Read it and summon the winged monkeys for help."

Good Witch Glinda's hands hovered over me with uncertainty. "Help. What does this thing want?"

"Ah," said Scarecrow. "I think I can interpret Toto's actions."

I don't know why Scarecrow felt the need to interpret me. I had enunciated my barks clearly, as I always did.

"Please do," said Good Witch Glinda, leaning back away from me, her eyes wide and hands in the air.

"It's obvious that Toto wants to dump Dorothy so he can remain here with you and be attended to by beautiful Good Witch Glinda Soldiers day and night and therefore he is offering you a gift in return."

"Dump me!" Dorothy fumed, folding her arms over her chest, and glaring at me.

"Either that," Scarecrow offered an alternative interpretation to Dorothy, "or Toto is attempting to give the Golden Cap to the Good Witch Glinda so she may summon the winged monkeys for herself and use them as she pleases."

"That had better be the case." Dorothy eyed me sternly and gave a little stomp of her foot.

"In any event," said Scarecrow to Dorothy, "the Good Witch Glinda should claim the Golden Cap because it is no longer of any use to you."

"Fine," said Dorothy, still fuming.

I picked up the Golden Cap in my mouth again and bobbed my head up and down, indicating to Good Witch Glinda to take it. She was hesitant at first, but finally, she grabbed it, looked it over, and said, "How charming."

"It is ruff-ruff," we all replied. "Charming ruff."

"That's what I said." Good Witch Glinda shrugged.

"No ruff. The charms ruff-ruff," we tried to explain. "They're inside the rim of the Golden Cap ruff-ruff!"

Good Witch Glinda located the charms and asked, "Do I just read them?"

"First, you'll need to get off your high horse, I mean throne, so you can do some hopping on one leg as you repeat the charms out loud," explained Dorothy. "When the winged monkeys arrive, you can use the three commands they allow you to send my three companions where each of them wants to go. After that, it's adios amigos as far as the winged monkeys and the charms of the Golden Cap are concerned."

Good Witch Glinda, after memorizing the charm, removed her crown and placed the Golden Cap snug on her head. As she stood to step out onto the floor, I fell from her lap at Dorothy's feet. "By the way, what's that thing?" she pointed at me.

Dorothy bent and picked me up and held me tight in her arms. "This is Toto, my dog, and he's going with me. Or else!" she added, glaring at me again. I licked her face.

Like it or not I was heading back to Kansas. If I wasn't so loyal to Dorothy, I might have refused to go. What better life could there be for a dog than living here and being groomed daily by one or all of the beautiful Good Witch Glinda Soldiers? Yet, my lot in life was caring for Dorothy and making her laugh and I was determined to remain her best friend to the end, no matter where it took us. Even Omaha, heaven forbid!

"Now that you can summon the winged monkeys to send my friends over the buttheads," said Dorothy, "can you explain how I can get home to Kansas using my sparkly shoes?"

"Simply state your destination while tapping your heels together three times," answered Good Witch Glinda, one leg up in the air, ready to recite the inscription in the Golden Cap. "Then, like magic, three steps forward will carry you away in an instant."

However, before Dorothy tapped her sparkly shoes, she turned to our companions and bade each a farewell.

Scarecrow shook Dorothy's hand repeatedly while thanking her for helping him get his head stuffed with brains. When Dorothy finally pulled her hand away, she turned to hug Tin Woodman. Tears flowed from his eyes and Dorothy worked hard to dry them before his joints rusted. Then it was Lion's turn and, after a tender hug, he growled, "Great!"

Then each, in turn, patted me on the head and I found myself too choked up to bark anything.

While Good Witch Glenda muttered the charm and hopped on one foot, Dorothy closed her eyes and murmured, while tapping her heels three times, "Sparkly shoes, I want to go home to Aunt Em and Uncle Henry in Kansas." Holding me tightly in her arms, she took three steps forward, and in a dizzying flash; we were off.

NO PLACE LIKE HOME

Before we knew it, Dorothy and I landed right behind Aunt Em.
"Ruff," I greeted her. Startled, Aunt Em nearly jumped out of her muddy boots.

Turning around, she gasped for air while holding one hand to her heart. After a few gulps of air, she looked Dorothy over. "Where have you been and where are your shoes?"

Dorothy looked down at her feet which were now shoeless. "The sparkly shoes, they're gone. I must've lost them in flight."

"I don't know what you're talking about, but you can save the chatter for later," said Aunt Em, resting a pitch-fork over her shoulder. "Your Uncle Henry built a new house and your food is on the table getting cold. Go in and find something to put on your feet before you step on a rusty nail." Then, taking a whiff of me, she added, "When you have a chance, make sure to bathe that mutt. He smells to high heaven."

"Ruff," I barked sarcastically. "It's great to see you, too."

"Does the new house have a mantle?" asked Dorothy, looking at the basket that seemed never to leave the crook of her arm.

"Certainly," said Aunt Em. "Over the fireplace where it belongs."

Dorothy sat me down on the ground and I followed her into our brand-new house.

There was a plate of food on the table in the middle of the room and a dish of cold dog food on the floor by the door, but it was toward the mantle over the fireplace that Dorothy headed. I followed Dorothy and sat next to her as she reached into her basket. One by one, she took out the porcelain figurines and carefully arranged them on the mantle.

Then, as she turned to the table, the tiny porcelain dairymaid stuck her pink porcelain tongue out at Dorothy's back and froze rock solid in that pose.

As Dorothy sat, I put my nose to my dish and pushed it next to her chair, but before either of us took a bite, she reached down, picked me up and sat me on her lap, and looked at me.

"I've been thinking, Toto," she said and I began to worry. "There's no place like home, but still I think we need to get out and see other lands."

"Ruff," I agreed with her. Although our adventures in the Land of Oz were at times frightful and dangerous, it was still much more exciting and colorful than Kansas.

"I don't suppose we can count on another cyclone to carry us away." Dorothy was puzzled and then said, "I wonder where those sparkly shoes flew off to."

"Ruff-ruff-ruff," I suggested, tilting my head at the fields outside the window.

Dorothy gave a nod, agreeing with me. "After we eat, we'll do some searching about in the fields. They must be out there somewhere. Though, if we do find them, wherever shall we go?"

I glanced down at my dish of cold dog food. I ate better in the Land of Oz so it has to be someplace where they serve decent food for creatures of all sorts.

Dorothy sat me down and dug her fork into her food, but stopped and looked at it. "Strangely, I've lost my appetite," she sighed.

I sniffed at my bowl of dog food and nodded my head, having lost my appetite, too.

Pushing her plate of food away from her, Dorothy looked around at the interior of our new house. A box on the floor by a rocking chair caught her attention and she jumped to her feet, ran over to it, and sat her bottom on the cold floor. I sat next to her as she reached into the box and took out a stack of items unfamiliar to me. She picked a few from the top of the stack and turned it toward me.

"Time Magazines," she said. As she looked through them, she placed each one on the floor in front of me. Most of these so-called Time Magazines had pictures of humans, some smiling, some frowning, and others looking stiff and grumpy.

I was getting bored with it all and I was about to turn away when Dorothy held one up to me and said, "Look, Toto, here's a picture you might like."

On the front of this particular magazine were two dogs sitting at a table in a restaurant while two men, one skinny, and the other fat, danced behind them with their mouths wide open.

Dorothy explained, "The fat one is dressed as a waiter and he's playing the accordion. The skinny man with the tall, round hat that is puffed up on top I'm sure is a chef and he's strumming a guitar of some sort and they're both singing." Then she pointed to the dish in front of the dogs. "That's a big plate of spaghetti smothered in a thick, red sauce and those round things on top of it are juicy meatballs. Now, if you will notice, the male dog is pushing a meatball with his nose across the plate over to the female dog. Isn't that nice?"

Nice or not, that pile of spaghetti with juicy meatballs looked delicious. I tilted my head, wagged my tail, and panted with my tongue hanging out to one side of my mouth, unable to take my eyes off it. It did look like a very good place to visit.

"Now where is this?" Dorothy placed a finger on the side of her cheek and contemplated the picture. "If they're eating spaghetti they must be in an Italian restaurant." Suddenly her eyes grew wide and she said excitedly, "If we can find those sparkly shoes I know where we should go next. Italy!"

THE END

Did you love *Toto Reveals the True Story*? Then you should read *Mystery of the Missing Parents*[1] by Dennis Sanchez!

[2]

Wooden puppet children seek the help of detectives, Dorothy, blind Scarecrow, and his seeing eye dog, Toto, in finding their missing parents that were carved into self-lighting Greek god candlesticks. Their travels take them from Italy to the belly of the Whale Inn in New Bedford, England where an uproarious confrontation takes place with pirates of the Caribean.

After Dorothy and Toto returned to Kansas, Tin Woodman was left in charge of the Winkies in the castle of the Wicked Witch of the West after she was dissolved. One day, in the woods, Tin Wooden comes across a tree and hears voices in it. The voices explain they are a family by name of Cottonwood. Realizing the voices are parents and

---

1. https://books2read.com/u/4DgLgP

2. https://books2read.com/u/4DgLgP

three children, a girl, and two boys, Tim Wooden decides to free them from the tree by chopping them into five logs. A cyclone scoops up the logs and carries them to Italy where a sculptor carves the children into wooden puppets and the parents into self-lightening Greek god candlesticks. When the parents go missing, the children seek the help of detectives, Dorothy, blind Scarecrow, and his seeing-eye dog, Toto, in finding their parents. Their travels take them from Italy to the belly of the Whale Inn in New Bedford, England. There they come across Lion and Tin Woodmen. What follows is an uproarious confrontation with pirates of the Caribbean in the belly of the wooden Whale Inn.

Read more at https://damfinowriter.webnode.com/.

About the Author

Dennis Sanchez was born and raised in Los Angeles and has remained a resident since. He received his BA in Communications from California State University, Fullerton, where he focused on journalism, film, and television production, and stop-motion animation. As a senior in college, he received the Student Editing Award from the Hollywood chapter of the American Cinemas Editors Guild and spent his internship on the set of Little House on the Prairie at Paramount Studios.

Now retired, he concentrates his energy on fiction, both humorous and serious content.

Email: damfinoswriter@gmail.com

Read more at https://damfinowriter.webnode.com/.